# BRAND

## BROTHERHOOD PROTECTORS WORLD

## LEANNE TYLER

Twisted Page Press LLC

BROTHERHOOD PROTECTORS

ORIGINAL SERIES BY ELLE JAMES

*Dedication*

*Pax and Michele – thanks to your support, counsel, and the lunches.*

## ACKNOWLEDGMENTS

I'd like to give thanks to Kelly Rivers who was instrumental in the creation of Brand Chambers, Will McLeod, Carly Manning, Simone Reid, Jules Gentry, and Colleen Summers when we were writing together in 2003. Characters never die even if story ideas do. Big thanks for her allowing me to resurrect these characters and put them into this new series with her blessing.

# CHAPTER 1

CARLY MANNING STOOD at the bar, threw back her head and downed her second tequila shooter. The aftershock riveted through her body like a good orgasm. Not that she'd had one in a long while, but that could change tonight. After all, her friends had brought her to the Pied Piper so she could put her failed marriage behind her and move on.

*Like a one-night stand was the answer.*

*Maybe it was.*

All she needed to do was get a little liquid courage into her system and find the right man to go home with tonight.

Without pause, she plunked the empty glass on the bar. "Hit me again."

"Woohoo, that's the spirit." Simone danced with a chrome pole on a nearby eight by eight stage. Her reddish-brown hair shimmered in the overhead spotlights.

Carly grinned, leaning her back against the bar as she watched her friend. Simone was the free spirit of their group. Long legs, tiny waist, nice chest, and creamy skin tone. She was a real beauty, and men had trouble not watching her when she walked into the room. Simone shimmied against the pole, her spring dress rose higher and higher with each move.

Colleen swayed at the jukebox, her blonde ponytail bobbing to the music. Their quiet friend wore a sedate blouse and skirt and flats. Jules lounged at their table, her feet propped up, nursing a single-malt scotch on the rocks. Her rebel-without-a-cause attitude didn't fool Carly for a moment. She knew her friend carried the load of the world on her feminine shoulders tonight. It would take more than a drink to wash away Jules' worries over budget cuts at the youth center. Despite this, her friend shook her spiky, dark brown hair in time to the music.

"You guys look like a hair color commercial," Carly said, laughing.

"Look who's talking." Jules turned in her direction and gestured with her drink. "You're the one who looks like something out of Victoria's Secret catalog."

"What? I'm well covered. Besides, you all picked it out." She did feel a little exposed by the white clinging tank that only reached her midriff. But the light-weight faux leather jacket and matching black short shorts shielded her. The latter covered all the essentials and did marvelous things for her legs. And the black, silver studded, open toe, mid-ankle boots she wore added three more inches to her height.

Simone left the pole and danced over to the bar, looking her in the eye. "The whole point of this evening is to get you out of your comfort zone. You're the one that wanted a change in your life. We wanted it to be a liberation, now that you're divorced from that control freak Justin Porter."

Carly downed the next shot of tequila, not wanting to think about her divorce from Justin. It had taken two long years of him fighting tooth and nail to keep her under his thumb. Yet, she'd received the divorce despite Justin's high priced attorney's stall tactics. "Another one bartender," she said.

Colleen rushed over and reached for Carly's hand. "Pace yourself and don't forget to drink water. You don't want to find yourself flat on the floor," She warned with a sweet smile, leading her back to their table.

Simone followed with a tray containing a pitcher of water and the next round of drinks. They toasted Carly and her newfound freedom. She couldn't complain if her friends thought she needed a hot-to-trot divorcée party. It wasn't every day she could gather with them and celebrate her liberation as a single woman. After seven years of trying to be the dutiful and proper wife of Justin Porter, Carly deserved a little fun. She'd already given herself permission if she found something she had to have to go for it.

Not that she would, but she'd given herself permission anyway. That was the tiny first step she needed. Justin had taken away all her rights soon after they married fresh out of college. He'd started with her self-esteem and confidence. Despite her degree as an interior designer, he'd convinced her she didn't need a career. His argument had been that because of his job as an attorney, he could well provide for them. His ambitions to excel at his law firm and in the political arena meant Carly hosting afternoon teas and luncheons at the country club. He also wanted her involved in fundraising events on a regular basis. Not to mention loathsome dinner parties they'd had to attend to ensure he kept up the appearance as a team player. That left no time for her to have a career of her own.

She couldn't remember how many times she'd berated herself for allowing him to show her off like a trophy wife. She'd tolerated patronizing smiles and smarmy propositions from his colleagues. But, she kept quiet. Her parents had raised her that marriage was a partnership in and out of the bedroom. She should do her part to be the meek and accommodating wife if she wanted a successful marriage. Her father was an attorney as well so she'd grown up knowing what that was like and the sacrifices her mother had made. So Carly knew what to expect before she'd married. But in the end, she found she'd needed more in her marriage. To her, making a marriage work meant both parties worked to make it successful, not one. Carly felt she was doing all the work, while Justin reaped all the rewards.

It had taken her five years to get fed up with her lifestyle. Her miraculous friends helped wake her up from the nightmare of her marriage. They stood by her even during the long two-year fight to finally be free of Justin Porter. While the ordeal had estranged her from her parents. That was the one thing she had not counted on.

A new song began to play, which got Jules on her feet and dancing with Colleen and Simone. Their little party was drawing quite the crowd at the Pied Piper tonight. The bar drew the sort of gathering that Carly had always wanted to be a part of, but didn't fit with her proper upbringing. Her friends' groupies varied from frat boys to the rising executives from downtown. They urged her to join them. Carly decided to sit this one out as she sipped water and enjoyed looking at the separation of styles. Martini-drinking yuppies sat on one end of the bar. Those doing shooters or drinking from longnecks sat on the other. Her upbringing should have put her with the martini drinkers. Yet tonight, she'd placed herself at the other end. A place she decided was having far more fun and was calling to her to let her hair down.

She downed her fourth or was it her fifth tequila? She wasn't sure, but who was counting anyway? And went back to the bar, clunking the glass on the hardwood. She smiled at the bartender.

"Another one?"

"This girl deserves some fun tonight." She leaned into the edge of the bar.

"What kind of fun did you have in mind?" a deep voice inquired from over her shoulder.

A warmth flowed through her at his nearness. She whirled around a little too fast to see if he looked as yummy as he sounded. The colors of the room blurred together and she closed her eyes, defeating the purpose of looking at the man.

"Grab hold of my arms and breathe deep," he instructed as he stepped forward to steady her.

She did as he asked. Instant steadiness returned. Fear washed over her at having a total stranger in her personal space. Her eyes flew open in a flash and she let go of his arms. "Sorry. I forgot turning around so fast makes me dizzy."

He grinned, showing perfect white teeth in the overhead lighting. She longed for the long-haired man to move out of her personal space. Yet, she didn't want to appear rude. He wasn't exactly what she had in mind as her prize for the night so she'd keep looking. "Thanks again for your help. Can I get you a drink?"

"Sure. I'll have what you're having."

Carly looked back at the bartender. "Add one to my tab for him."

The bartender nodded, turned away and came back a few seconds later with two ice-filled glasses of water.

"Hey, what's the meaning of this?" the man said, letting go of Carly and planting his hands on the bar in front of him.

"I'm cutting her off," the bartender explained. "If she can't stand without you steadying her for as long as you did, then she doesn't need another shot of tequila. Now if you'd like one, I'll be happy to serve you."

Carly snickered. She took the glass of water and raised it in salute to the men. Then she sauntered back to her friends, feeling lucky that punches weren't thrown.

"What have you been up to?" Simone asked when the song ended and her friends settled back at the table.

"Escaping the rough hands of the long-haired man at the bar. I've had enough shooters for one night."

"We need food." Colleen picked up the small menu on the table and rattled off the appetizers. "Let's get the slider platter and the loaded cheesy bacon fries."

"Girl, because you can eat like that and not gain an ounce, doesn't mean we're all blessed with your genes," Simone said.

Carly rolled her eyes at Simone because she was tall

and lean, without an ounce of fat on her size three body.

"Live a little," Jules said, snatching the menu from Colleen. "I'll go order and be right back with a round of beer for us all. Longnecks or a pitcher?"

"Longnecks."

Jules returned with four bottles.

"Let's toast Carly and her new life," Jules announced, handing out the bottles. "Isn't that what we're here for?"

"Here. Here." Colleen raised her bottle.

Carly blushed and tried to hide the fact by drinking her beer.

The waitress came shortly after with the sliders and the fries. The four talked, scarfed down the food, and then the girls showered Carly with gifts.

Simone squealed, stomping her feet happily on the floor as she produced a small tiger print gift bag with black tissue paper. "I hope you have lots of fun with these."

Carly eyed the bag for a moment, holding her breath. Sticking her hand inside, she pulled out furry, leopard print handcuffs.

"This one's from me," Colleen said, sitting down another small, sparkly gift bag with bright tissue paper.

"Is there a theme to these gifts?" Carly asked.

"Yeah, that you use them," Simone said.

The girls giggled as Carly reached inside and pulled out a handful of glow in the dark condoms. She held her hand suspended above the bag for a few seconds before she dropped them back inside. Then she reached for Jules sedate white gift bag with pink tissue.

"Do I even want to look inside this one? It looks all innocent, but that means it's deceptive because it's coming from you, counselor."

Jules shrugged. "Depends on how adventurous you are."

Taking a deep breath, Carly pulled out the pink tissue paper. She unwrapped a biker babe leather thong teddy and whip set. "Good heavens."

The girls laughed some more as Carly's cheeks flamed. When she recovered, she wrapped the items back in the tissue and stuffed them into the gift bag again. After placing the other two gift bags inside of Jules' bag, she stowed all the gifts inside her large black bag. It was more than her purse. It contained a change of clothes in case she didn't go home tonight.

"You guys didn't have to do this or bring these here…tonight. You could have given them to me at my little apartment."

Colleen shook her head. "That place is so small. I swear, my linen closet is bigger."

Simone snorted, made a face, and then covered her nose and mouth with both hands.

"Sorry you don't approve, but it was all I could afford. I wasn't awarded alimony."

"Which is asinine!" Jules stood up. "That is the one thing about your divorce I don't agree with. How could the judge grant it without awarding you alimony? Justin Porter comes from money. Didn't one of his ancestors found that country club he belongs to?"

Carly nodded. "One of the first members. But his family doesn't like to brag."

Simone snorted again. "Is that why he mentioned it so often when you were first dating?"

"Did he?"

"Yes." Jules tossed a used napkin on the table. "He got the house, while you moved into a tiny apartment that you can't afford without any support. You have no job. Your parents aren't speaking to you because you left him, it's—"

"I have a job interview next week now that the divorce is final and I can focus on not going to court every day."

"The legal system is screwy. Where is justice in the world?" Jules continued to fume.

Colleen patted their friend on the shoulder. "It'll be okay. The youth center will find money somewhere to support the programs for the kids. There have been budget cuts before and the center has survived."

Jules kicked the leg of a nearby chair. "Not like these cuts."

"I'm sorry, Jules, I hadn't realized it had gotten so bad this week," Simone said. "Someone should have let me know when I got back in town from my business trip."

Jules shook her head, sitting back down. "Enough

about me. It's Carly's night out and we still have plenty of time before the bar closes. Another round of drinks? A round of pool?"

"A little pole dancing for our divorcee?" Simone suggested, getting to her feet and trying to persuade Carly to join her up on the stage. "You're not going to find Mr. Right Now if you stay hidden behind a table all night. You gotta get out on the dance floor and move your moneymaker."

Carly shook her head and held up her hands. "Guys, please, stop. I've had more than my limit of alcohol for one night and dancing when I'm feeling like this is not going to be good. I won't attract anything but a bucket and a mop."

"Okay, then what would you like to do?" Colleen asked, reaching out and taking her hands in hers. "We're here to please."

"I want to spend time with my besties. Is that so wrong? I know you think I need to have a hot night out, but have I drawn a man to me tonight? Well, other than Mr. Longhair guy, but you know. Have you been asked out? No. Is there something wrong with us?"

"We're sending off the wrong vibes," Colleen said. "We're woman, hear us roar, but stand your distance buster."

Jules smirked. "You got that right."

"More the reason you need to get up on the stage and shake your bootie." Simone went to the jukebox, selected Firefly before going to the stage and proceeded to sway and gyrate.

Colleen ran to join her, laughing. They joined hands, raising their arms in a slow-motion wave.

"What do you say, Carly?" Jules asked.

Carly shrugged. "What the hell. Let's get it on with Ed Sheeran."

As they joined their friends, a few of the guys in the bar sauntered over and began dancing with them as well.

When a slow song played, Carly danced with a cute frat boy five years her junior, but she wasn't about to quibble over age. It was a dance after all. It wasn't like he was taking her home tonight. She'd come here alone and she'd already made up her mind that she was going home alone. It had been a good thought that she'd meet someone, but that hadn't happened. Another night out with her friends might turn out different?

"Thanks for the dance," she said.

"No, thank you," the guy said, winking at her before he headed back toward his friends at the bar.

"Woohoo, looks like Carly found her a young one." Simone hovered near her shoulder.

"He's not my type."

"Do you even know what your type is anymore?"

Carly shrugged, not having an answer to that question.

A bell rang near the bar and everyone stopped what they were doing. The bartender climbed up on the wooden surface and announced, "Last call. We'll be closing in fifteen."

Wolf howls and cheering came from the group of frat boys and then a round of slaps on the backs of some of the guys.

"Wonder what that was all about?" Jules arched a brow. "Well, I hate to bail, but I have an early morning meeting."

"On a Saturday?" Simone questioned.

Jules nodded. "With all the budget cuts we have to figure out how we're going to keep the few programs we can from tanking."

"See you. Call if you need to talk." Colleen made a sad face before hugging her. When she pulled away she looked at Carly and Simone. "I need to hit the ladies before we leave."

"Okay. We'll wait for you at the bar," Carly told her. Then she leaned toward Simone. "I want to thank the bartender for cutting me off earlier. He saved me from making a fool out of myself."

"Are you sure that is the only reason you are wanting to talk to him?" Simone cooed.

Carly ignored her friend and slid onto an empty barstool.

"Come back for another shot?" the bartender asked.

"No. This girl knows when she's had her limit. You were right to cut me off when you did. I wanted to thank you for doing that earlier. I'm Carly, by the way."

"Phil. And it was my pleasure to give you an out to

get away from that guy. I could tell you didn't look comfortable with him touching you."

"No, I didn't. Thanks again."

"Are you single?" Simone asked. "Carly's recently divorced."

"Nope." Phil held up his olive-toned hand sporting a wide titanium band.

Damn. Carly hadn't even noticed that earlier. He was nice looking too. His arms showed he worked out when he wasn't tending bar. Why were all the decent men taken?

"You'll have to excuse my friend here. She doesn't think before she speaks when she's been drinking."

"That's okay. It happens all the time in my line of work." Phil walked away to take care of a server at the other end of the bar.

"Too bad he's taken. He's hot. I'd do him in a heart-beat," Simone said.

"There isn't much you wouldn't do when you've been drinking."

"Ouch. Let's not get our claws out. I'm trying to have some fun. Lighten up. Where'd fun Carly go?"

Carly glanced at her. "Sorry, but it's late and I'm getting a headache. I'm not accustomed to having all this kind of *fun*."

The door to the bar opened. A young, leather-clad man with a red rolled bandana tied around his dark head ran into the bar. Two more young men followed him wearing jeans and dark t-shirts. They both had snake tattoos up and down their arms and necks that cried gang relations. It wasn't clear what their purpose was coming into the bar so late, nor did they approach Phil to order a drink. They meandered around as if interested in the jukebox or getting a table.

The place was pretty empty by this point and a couple made a hasty exit. Carly began to wonder what was taking Colleen so long in the ladies room. There wasn't a line that long this time of night. And she hoped her friend hadn't gotten sick from the alcohol they'd consumed.

"We better get out of here." Simone grabbed her arm and pulled her off the bar stool, but Carly shook her head.

"We can't. We're waiting on Colleen."

She'd barely spoken when she saw Phil reach under the counter and pick up a baseball bat and lower it toward his knee.

Simone's protest came out like a mouse's high pitched squeak when the trio headed back toward the bar.

"What can I do for you fellas?" Phil asked.

"Your money." The guy in the leather pulled a .45 on Phil.

Carly blinked and thought she was going to be sick. She'd never been this close to death before.

"Excuse me?" Phil didn't flinch nor did he raise the baseball bat either. For a man with a gun in his face, he was being very calm.

"Your money, mother fucker. Open up that fucking drawer and give us all your money or you and the rest of these assholes are dead."

Gasps and murmurs filled the place. It became deathly quiet when the other two pulled out their guns and pointed them at the patrons as well. One pointed his shiny silver .45 at Simone and immediately pulled the trigger, but no bullet fired. He laughed his ass off when she sank to the floor whimpering.

Carly wanted to comfort her friend, but she was afraid to move. She didn't want to set the guy off and have him pull the trigger in her face. There had been no reason for him to point the gun at Simone or pull the trigger in the first place, but he had. Clearly this guy was not stable. Also, she wondered what might happen to Phil if he didn't open up the cash drawer and give these thugs the money.

She prayed he wouldn't do something foolish, like reach for the bat, but he did. He swung it in one fluid motion, trying to take them out in one powerful swing. They didn't see it coming. He took down two, but one got a shot off that hit Phil center of his chest. The force of the bullet sent him crashing back against the bottles of booze display. The wall of glass behind him shattered into millions of pieces all around him.

Screams mingled with laughter ricocheted throughout the place. The shooter sounded like a crazed hyena as he got to his feet.

Carly ducked and found Simone wasn't on the floor

crying but she was on her cell, calling for help. Carly gave her friend a thumbs up. Then she crawled to the opening in the bar to get to Phil to check on whether he was alive or dead. She was thankful that Colleen was still in the ladies and hadn't had to witness what they had.

## CHAPTER 2

BRANDON "BRAND" Chambers zipped up his tactical bag in preparation for heading to the airport. It had been a good week of presentations to the Chicago PD, featuring how Hank Patterson's Brotherhood Protectors could aid law enforcement in metro cities. This was another way Patterson was branching out. Giving his wounded warriors another avenue back into society.

While his three teammates finished up with their gear, Brand walked to the door of the presentation room to speak with Hawkeye, a former SEAL buddy.

Hawkeye, who was now a police commander in one of the many districts of Chicago, greeted Brand with a quick nod. "Thanks again, Brand, for showing us what the Brotherhood Protectors can do. We could use a team like yours if we could find the funds. We don't always have the resources to provide protection to all citizens in our districts. If we could call on your team to do it that would free up our officers to do their job."

"Unfortunately we come at a price," Brand said. "With our level of expertise, add in a cost of living, plus the expense of surveillance equipment. It all adds up."

"I get it."

A detective walked into the room. "Commander Burns, I need to speak to you for a moment."

Hawkeye touched Brand on the arm. "If you can hang for five minutes, I'd like to run an idea by you to take back to Hank. I promise I won't keep you hanging long, but I need to see what this is about."

"Sure." Brand did an about-face and returned to his teammates.

"So are we ready to head to the airport?" Liam 'Don Juan' Donovan slung his bag onto his shoulder.

"No. Hawkeye wants us to stay a while longer."

Wyatt Kincaid checked his watch. "We're already cutting it close on catching our flight. Don Juan and Loverboy might be able to sweet talk the attendant at the gate into letting us onto the flight. They can't get us through security checkpoints any quicker than necessary."

Will 'Loverboy' McLeod punched him in the arm. "I'll have you know our skills come in handy as much as your ability to deal with PTSD victims, so don't knock it."

"Don't worry, guys," Brand said. "We'll still make our flight, even if we have to get a police escort to the airport. Let's double check to make sure we have all our gear secured."

The team grumbled, but they did the check anyway. They knew he was a stickler about their equipment after what happened to him in Afghanistan.

His teammate hadn't packed their bag properly before they went into theater. It was a rookie mistake for a seasoned SEAL. It cost Joe his life. It left Brand carrying a piece of shrapnel around in his chest—too close to his pulmonary artery. He wasn't cleared for active duty once he'd recovered from the gunshot wound. In retrospect, Joe shouldn't have gone on that mission. His head hadn't been in the game. It was too soon after his wife left him, but Joe had been stubborn and claimed he was fine when he wasn't.

Brand closed his eyes and ran a hand up the back of his neck to the top of his head. He still broke out into a cold sweat whenever he thought about that time in his life. When he opened his eyes Hawkeye was coming toward him with a grim expression on his face.

"Bad news?" Brand asked.

"In my line of duty, that's all I get." Hawkeye placed his hands on his slender hips, shaking his head. "There was an attempted robbery at a bar on the waterfront. Bartender dead. The shooter was beaten with a base-ball bat by a patron. I'm going to need your team's help, Brand. I've got four witnesses who need individualized protection. Don't worry. I already called Hank, and he's given you the okay to stay as long as I need you for this. This will serve two-fold. It will provide the protection we need and it will show those higher up your services in action."

Brand started to speak, but Hawkeye held up a hand, cutting him off.

"Before you protest, think about all the good staying will be doing for the people of Chicago."

Brand grinned. "I wasn't going to protest. I was only going to say we'll need to change our flights."

"Let my administrative assistant handle it for you. She'll get you an open-ended deal with the city paying for the change fee. It's the least we can do." Hawkeye slapped him on the back.

"And I'll let you tell my men we aren't going home to Montana."

Hawkeye chuckled.

LIGHTS FLASHING AND SIRENS BLASTING, the two police SUVs charged through the night to the waterfront. His team took the news that they had an assignment from Hawkeye without remark. He'd have been shocked if they had, knowing their creed was to protect and serve where needed.

They arrived on the scene within minutes. Hawkeye led the way. He stopped a few feet from where a woman argued with a detective who refused her entry into the bar.

"You don't understand. I was in there earlier with my friends. If I hadn't had to leave to catch the "L," I would have been with them when the shooting happened. I know they're still in there. I need to check to make sure they're okay."

Hawkeye turned to Brand. "According to my report, that's Jules Gentry. One of your men needs to stay with her. As I understand it, she spotted the getaway car. I'll explain to the detective that your man is taking over."

Brand nodded. "McLeod. She's yours. Find out what you can about what she knows and make sure no reporters get near her."

"You got it."

"Donovan, Kincaid, follow me," Brand ordered, leading them into the Pied Piper bar. He grunted at the name.

The scene inside was what he expected. The overhead lights were at full throttle. There were tables with knocked over chairs. Shattered glass mirror and broken glass bottles littered the floor. For a crime scene, it was a madhouse with all the people walking through the evidence. There were officers, detectives, CSI, and the coroner on the scene doing their jobs. A gurney with a black body bag was ready for the van.

Crime scene tape cordoned off detained patrons on the left side of the bar. On the ride over, Hawkeye had described their assignment and the women. Brand narrowed in on two of the women huddled together at a table. They leaned toward each other, talking. One was a blonde in a leather jacket and short shorts exposing long, sexy legs. He was a stickler for blondes with long legs. He felt his throat go dry and a familiar stirring of desire uncoil. But then he recalled she had taken down the gang member with the baseball bat. And he wondered what had made her snap to swing that bat so hard or that many times? He mentally shook himself, not allowing his thoughts to go there. He was here to do a job and nothing more. The other was a redhead in a short dress. Not his type.

"I'll take the redhead," Donovan said before Brand could issue assignments.

Brand smirked. "Of course you will. Remember she's an assignment, not your date for the weekend. You will keep your libido in check, Don Juan."

"Hey now, you know I'm not a lover boy like McLeod. The guys in my unit only nicknamed me that because it went with Donovan."

"But you do have a way with the ladies," Wyatt pointed out.

Donovan punched his friend in the arm. "You're not helping man. You're not helping."

"So do I get the blonde?" Wyatt asked.

Brand considered that for half a second but shook his head. "No. She's mine."

Hawkeye walked up. "Good. I see you've found your assignments. The blonde is Carly Manning, the one who used the bat on the shooter. The other is Simone Reid. She had a gun pointed at her, fired, but there was no bullet. We're not sure if that means the gang has targeted her or not. That's something we'll be checking into. Whoever is covering her can dig deeper from her point of view on it as well?

"Can do." Donovan nodded.

"Kincaid, I understand you're good with PTSD victims."

"That's right, Commander Burns."

"Then come with me." The two walked a short distance, then stopped. "Special Victims was called. We had more than a shooting in this bar tonight. Your assignment is being loaded into a bus headed to Chicago Medical Center. I'll get you a ride with them to the hospital. Stay with her and make sure she's treated with the best care. We're not clear to what extent her injuries range. We aren't even sure if there was penetration. Likewise, we do not know if the incident was random or related to the gang. It's your job to find out as much as possible without causing her more stress."

Wyatt nodded and then made eye contact with Brand. "I'll be in touch."

Brand nodded, then motioned for Donovan to follow him. "Let's go talk to the girls."

Donovan followed him, stopping in front of the women. Brand waited for them to acknowledge his presence, which took longer than he expected. But they both finally looked his way.

"Can we help you?" the redhead said.

"I'm Brand Chambers and my partner here is Liam Donovan. We'd like to speak with you both if you don't mind."

"We've already talked to the police and the detectives. How many more people do we have to talk to tonight before we can go home?" she asked.

"Moi," Donovan said. "And I can assure you if you do, I'll get you out of here and to your home as soon as I can."

"How do we know you aren't some Jo Blow who walked from off the street?"

"We're part of a new task force and have been assigned to protect you," Brand said, flashing her his Brotherhood Protectors Badge and his Chicago PD visitor's badge. Don Juan did the same.

The redhead nodded. "In that case. I'm Simone Reid. This is my friend Carly Manning."

"Hi." Carly looked at them with smeared mascara underneath her blue eyes. "Do you know how the gang member I hit with the bat is doing? No one will tell me anything other than he's transported to the hospital criminal ward."

Her hands were trembling as she spoke, and she placed them on the table in front of her. Simone wrapped an arm around her and hugged her close.

"What do you need to know so we can get out of here?" Simone asked again. She didn't seem to care who they were or how they were going to get them out of the bar as long as they got home that night. To

Brand, this didn't bode well. It showed him she was reckless, and he was glad he wasn't assigned to her.

Brand stepped forward and knelt down beside Carly. "What made you use the bat?"

Her head snapped around quick, but her eyes were blank looking. "He'd killed Phil. I'd crawled around through the entrance of the bar to see if there was a pulse and the man came upon me. He was threatening me with his gun. He claimed he would shoot me if I didn't get away from the body. I—I— snapped. Phil was the nicest man I had met in a long time. He'd protected me from myself when I'd had too much to drink earlier tonight. Then there was this thug. He came in and killed him for no reason. He—he was going to shoot me for no reason too. He had this hysterical laugh like a crazed animal. I'll never get that sound out of my head. What kind of a monster was he?"

A single tear ran down her cheek and Brand reached up to wipe it away with the pad of his thumb. Instead of wetness, he felt a jolt of electricity that almost knocked him off his feet. He rocked to a standing position.

"There isn't always an explanation for why people do what they do. It's getting late. Let's get you both out of here for the night. I'm sure if the police or detectives have any more questions for you, it can wait until the morning."

"Thank you," Carly said, reaching for a black bag that looked more like an overnight than a purse.

"Why don't you stay with me tonight," Simone suggested.

Carly nodded.

"Wait a minute ladies," Donovan said, waving his hand at them. "I'm afraid we can't let you do that. We're here to keep you both safe and the best way to do that is to keep you at two different locations."

"Wh-why do you think we need protecting?" Carly asked. "Do you think the gang will try to retaliate against me because I swung that bat at the shooter?"

"We aren't sure. But you did keep him from getting away with the other two."

"As we understand it, Simone, you had a gun pointed at you. That could have been random. But what if it wasn't? Could there have been a reason this particular gang would target you?" Donovan asked.

Simone's bottom lip began to tremble. She shook her head and bit her lip.

Donovan looked at Brand and they exchanged knowing looks. There was more there than she was willing to tell either of them at the moment.

"Okay ladies. As promised you've answered our initial questions and we're going to get you out of here for the night. Is there anything you'd like to know or do before we leave here?" Donovan asked.

Carly nodded. "Our friend Colleen. She went to the ladies and we haven't seen her since. No one will tell us anything. Can you find out what happened to her? Have they made her stay in there while they clear the crime scene out here like they've made us stay over here?"

"Possible," Donovan said. "But we'll check that out and see what we can find out for sure."

"What's her full name?" Brand asked.

"Colleen Summers. Why?" Simone asked. "She's not dead is she?"

"No. Nothing to that extreme," Donovan assured as Brand left to find Hawkeye.

He spotted the Commander talking to one of the detectives on the case on the opposite side of the bar.

"Everything okay?" Hawkeye asked.

"Fine. We're about to get the women out of here, but they are asking about their friend who was in the ladies room. Her name is Colleen Summers. I thought you'd want that information to the hospital if her purse went missing in the attack."

"Thanks. It was. You didn't tell them anything did you?"

"No. Donovan told them we'd investigate to see what we could learn. Any update on her condition yet?"

"Too soon."

"Can I at least tell them their friend is at the hospital getting checked out?"

Hawkeye thought for a moment. "The EMT was here checking them over so the bus was here, yea, that should be okay. But that we have no other info on why now."

"Gottcha. I assume we have use of the SUV cruisers?"

Hawkeye nodded. "Each driver is ready when you are. I got the women's addresses and your numbers so I will know how to reach you."

Brand walked back across the bar to where Donovan and the women waited. Both Carly and Simone stood as soon as they saw him.

"What did you learn?"

"Where is Colleen?" Their questions came at once.

"I found out that the bus that treated the patrons here tonight took your friend to Chicago Medical Center. She's alive."

The two hugged each other.

When they pulled apart, they looked at one another, and said in unison. "Jules."

"She's outside. Or she was when we arrived," Donovan said. "She was trying to get in here, but the detective wouldn't let her because it was a crime scene."

"Then we need to go outside and talk to her. Let her know we're okay," Simone said, grabbing her purse off the table. "You want to protect me, Mr. Donovan, then let's get a move on. I want to see Jules."

"She may not be there anymore. She's a witness and needed protecting too. One of our guys is with her. He may have already taken her home."

"One of your guys is with Jules? Why?" Carly asked, stepping toward Brand.

"She saw the getaway car. She heard the gunshots on her way to the "L" and came back to the bar."

"So now she is in danger too?" Carly asked.

Brand nodded.

"What a night."

## CHAPTER 3

"YOU'LL HAVE to forgive me for the smallness of my apartment. It's all I could afford after my divorce." Carly let Brand into her apartment. "If you want, I can give you the bedroom and take the sofa sleeper."

"I don't want to take your bed. The sofa sleeper is fine. I'm ex-military. I can sleep in pretty bad conditions."

"If you're sure?" she asked.

Brand nodded.

She showed him around the tiny apartment that reminded him of his private dorm room in college. He'd lucked up getting assigned to that renovated building instead of crammed into a room with three other roommates.

Carly fluttered from room to room showing him the place. When she gave him an extra blanket and pillow, he noticed that her legs had been bleeding.

"What happened to your legs?"

"Oh that. The EMTs checked me out and cleaned me up. It's where I crawled to Phil and the broken glass cut me. I was lucky none of the pieces got embedded in my flesh."

"Yeah, you were."

"Help yourself to anything in the kitchen. If you want something I don't have, we can get it tomorrow. Exactly how long do you think you'll be staying here?"

"I'm not sure. Until I'm told otherwise."

She nodded and chewed on her bottom lip, staring at him for a long moment, then she blinked and shook her head. "If you don't need anything else, I'll see you in the morning."

"Thanks. See you."

The door to the bedroom closed and Brand heard the door lock as he settled on the sofa to unwind. He grinned. Smart woman. Not that she had anything to worry about with him, but she didn't know that.

He was also glad she hadn't made a fuss about him taking her room. Sleeping out here allowed him to be near the front door if anyone tried to break in. He'd kept a watch as the SUV cruiser made its way through the semi-deserted streets to her apartment. When they arrived, he noticed a car parked across the street with a man inside snapping photos. Someone was watching her. Whether a local newspaper was already on the shooting tonight or something else. He couldn't be sure until he learned more about Carly Manning.

He waited until he was certain she'd gone to bed and was asleep before he took out his laptop. He set up a secured Wi-Fi portal through his encrypted cellphone and ran a background check on her. Within seconds he'd tapped into DMV records. He learned she'd recently changed her name from Porter back to her maiden name of Manning. He did a quick search of court records and learned her ex-husband was attorney Justin Porter. He tapped bank account records and saw that Carly had no money. Yet Justin had plenty and according to the divorce decree paid Carly no alimony. That was wrong.

Brand searched through the document again. Carly had claimed domestic abuse, but the judge had ruled it unfounded. There had been no corroborating arrests or judgments against Porter. No wonder Carly had locked the bedroom door. It explained why she'd been overprotective of the bartender because of his kindness. It was making more sense to Brand now.

He backed out of the records, made sure to leave no trace that he'd ever been there, and shut down his programs. As he did, a thought ran across his mind about the man watching downstairs. What if he wasn't related to the case tonight, but was a hired man for the ex-husband who still couldn't let go of Carly. If so, this could be an added complication to keeping her safe.

He put away his laptop and his equipment before unfolding the sofa bed. He double checked the lock on the door, and then he grabbed his toothbrush from his overnight bag. Heading to the bathroom, he had to find out all he could from Carly about Porter without alarming her. He'd even enlist the help of Donovan to get information about her from her friend Simone and report back to him.

CARLY TOSSED AND TURNED. The man waved the gun toward her and Simone before the man beside him fired. She screamed. The bullet moved in slow motion, hitting Phil square in the chest. He flew back against the mirrored liquor display. Shards of pebbled mirrored glass showered on her, Simone, and the gunmen, causing a blood bath. It was a horrific sight and she could taste the metallic tang of blood on her tongue.

Pounding on her door woke her and she sat up, tangled in her damp sheets, chilled to the bone.

"Carly. Carly are you okay?" An unfamiliar man's voice rattled her already frazzled nerves. For a moment she couldn't recall where she was or why there was a man in her apartment calling her name.

The taste of blood mingled with saliva almost made her gag as she remembered the events from last night and how she'd ended up bringing a stranger home with her. But not for the hot-to-trot one-night stand as intended by her friends. She rubbed her hand over her mouth and her lip stung from the contact, telling her she'd somehow bitten it in her sleep. The residue of blood on her hand, as well as the taste, made it clear she'd broken the skin.

Another knock came. "Carly, are you all right?"

Brand.

"Yes. Bad dream." She rubbed her hand on her sheet, then wiped the sleep from her eyes before she scrambled from the bed. She smoothed her hair away from her face and went to unlock her door. She only opened it a fraction so that she could peep out at him.

"Let me in. I need to check your room."

"No. I had a bad dream. That's all. I was reliving the nightmare of the shooting at the bar. I didn't mean to wake you."

"That may be true, but I still need to make sure no one broke through the window and is holding you at gun or knife point, forcing you to lie to me."

"I'm telling you the truth."

"I get that. Just let me in and then you can go back to bed."

"Seriously, I'm fine. Now go away."

"Then why is your lip bleeding?"

"I bit it in my sleep when I was dreaming."

"You need to put some ice on it."

"Duly noted."

"Now back away. I'm coming in."

She huffed, moving to the side so he could come in. He was barefoot but already wearing his tactical gear and had his gun drawn as he moved into the room checking it. She waited while he opened her closet, and then went into the bathroom. When he came out, he double checked the window. She burst out laughing.

"What's so funny?"

"You. Mr. Macho with the gun this morning."

"I'm doing my job." He put the gun in its shoulder holster.

"Protecting me from imaginary monsters?"

"Protecting you at all costs."

"From imaginary threats."

"It might not always be imaginary." He crossed his arms over his chest. "One morning you might wake up screaming because someone has really broken in that window, holding you captive. Then what? Wouldn't you want me breaking in that door and saving you from harm?"

Carly swallowed her mirth. "When you put it that way, yes."

"Did you know there is a man sitting in a car downstairs watching this building? He was there last night when we came in. He's still there this morning. I'd say he's been out there for some time watching your every move. Why don't you tell me about your ex-husband Justin Porter?"

"Wh-wh…how do you know his name?"

"I have my sources. I also know you got shafted in your divorce. That's why you're living in this respectable hole in the wall, but there's nothing to be ashamed of there. I get it. You wanted out and you didn't want anything that belonged to the bastard. But he may not be through with you if my hunch is right. So you see, I do have cause to check for 'imaginary threats'."

Carly wilted back against the wall. She licked her lips, getting a taste of blood again, and her legs began to collapse under her. She'd thought she'd been smart moving to this part of town, far enough away from Justin's reach.

Brand was there catching her before she hit the floor. He scooped her and carried her to the bed where he set her down. But instead of holding her, or trying to comfort her, he knelt in front of her, respecting her personal space.

The refusal of contact jolted her and it made her feel raw and rejected at the same time. The rational part of her brain was telling her this wasn't the reaction she should be having. He'd just told her there was a man outside that had been watching her. Likely had been watching her ever since she'd moved into her apartment. She'd thought when she divorced Justin Porter she'd cut all ties with him, but that wasn't the case.

"I didn't mean to alarm you. I wasn't going to tell you at all for that very reason, but it's clear you needed to know there's danger lurking outside."

"No. You should have told me. I-I'm glad you did. It was foolish for me to think that I could walk away without Justin Porter trying to keep some control over me. What can I do to stop him?"

"Unless he makes a threatening move against you, we can't get a restraining order against him. Nor can we make the man he's hired stop following you unless he does something illegal. I'm sure the man is a private investigator who knows the ins and outs of the legal system. He'll stay well within the borders of the law to protect himself."

"Then how do we stop him?"

"By staying alert at all times. You can't let your guard down."

*A prisoner in her own home again.*

Carly raked her fingers through her sleep tasseled hair and realized she must look a fright. But who cared? Brand was the one who'd barged into her bedroom to check it out because she'd had a bad dream.

"I-I think I want to be alone. I need to process this information. Help yourself to whatever food you can find in the kitchen."

He stood. "You aren't alone in this, Carly. I'm here with you. I'm here to protect you. Justin will not win. No matter what he tries."

"You don't know Justin Porter."

BRAND WENT into the kitchen and made a pot of coffee.

While it brewed, he searched for a Styrofoam cup and lid that Carly might have saved from a take-out order. He looked through all the cabinets before hitting pay dirt. Filling the cup with fresh brewed black, he headed downstairs to pay mister surveillance guy a visit.

It was clear as Brand crossed the street that the man was sleeping in his car. But who could blame him? It wasn't even six thirty on a Saturday morning. A few taps on the window startled the man awake and he jumped, alarm written all over his unshaven face. He started the car and rolled down the electric window.

"Can I help you, officer?"

"I'm not the police, but if I were I'd have you hauled in for stalking. Here's a cup of coffee. You look like you could use one. Tell Justin Porter to leave Carly alone."

"I don't know what you're talking about."

"Sure you don't. You're cover is blown, pal. I know you're here. She knows you're here. So take off before I call the cops on you."

"You have no grounds."

"No? Looks to me like you're living in your car. That's an offense in itself."

"You can't prove it."

"Empty food containers littering the car. The back seat looks like it's your dirty laundry hamper. When's the last time you showered? You were sleeping when I walked over here. I got it all on my cell." Brand held his phone for him to see. "So what is it going to be? Are you going to drive away or am I going to make a phone call to my buddy at Chicago PD?"

Without waiting for the man to answer, he dialed Hawkeye's personal line and stepped to the front of the car to get the license plate number.

"Burns here."

"It's Brand. Can you run a plate for me?"

"What? Do you think I'm your personal errand boy now?" Hawkeye chuckled.

"Humor me. I got a car parked outside Carly's apartment building. It was here last night and again this morning. The guy won't leave. I think her ex-husband is having her watched."

The man in the car backed up and swerved around Brand to leave the area.

Brand moved out of the street and onto the sidewalk.

"What's the plate?"

"FXJ 7854."

"Simon Ragsdale. Private Investigator. A former detective in the south side."

"You got all that from the plate?"

"No. I know the man. He doesn't come cheap either. Who is Carly's ex-husband?"

"Attorney Justin Porter."

Hawkeye whistled. "Now I get the connection between Ragsdale and Porter."

"Let me guess, you know Porter too?"

"I've heard of him. Comes from money. Country

club type. Chicago elite family. Makes you wonder what his ex-wife was doing down on the waterfront at the Pied Piper last night."

"Celebrating getting away from him. I ran a background check on her and learned she's newly divorced."

"Maybe so, but the Pied Piper is a far cry down from the country club scene."

"Did you see how she was dressed, Hawk? Leather jacket, a tank that barely covered her midriff, and short shorts? Not to mention those studded ankle boots. This woman was on the prowl last night."

"No, I didn't notice. I had other important matters on my mind than what the woman you are protecting was wearing. Are you worried you're in danger being so close to this woman? Afraid she might wrap you around her little finger if she bats her baby blues too many times?"

Brand grunted, then walked to the corner and crossed at the signal. "Me worried? Not on your life. I can handle her."

"Good. Glad to hear it."

"Besides, if you weren't looking, how'd you know she has blue eyes?"

"I didn't. It was a guess."

There was a pause on the line as Brand tried to regain face.

"Anything you want me to convey to the guys today? I'll be checking in with them later."

"We haven't located the other two gang members. Patrol units are still on the lookout for the make and model of the car that Jules Gentry spotted. The shooter was released from the hospital but will remain in police custody until he's arraigned Monday."

"Any word on Colleen?" Brand asked.

"You should be asking Kincaid, not me."

The phone went quiet on Hawkeye's end, and then Brand heard muffled voices, letting him know he was being shut out of another conversation.

"I've got to go, Brand. Keep me informed of any new occurrences on your end. And I'll call if there is anything urgent you need to know."

"Will do, Hawkeye."

## CHAPTER 4

CARLY DRIED her eyes and blew her nose, hating herself for giving into crying. Tears were no way to deal with Justin Porter. She knew that. She'd learned it long ago. Why had she given in this morning because Brand had told her a man was watching her apartment building? Which meant he'd been watching her without her being aware?

She smelled freshly brewed coffee and heard the front door close. Had Brand left? Where would he go? Wait…wasn't he supposed to be protecting her?

Still in her pajamas, she hurried to the living room, only to find it empty. He had left. Following the scent of coffee, she found half a pot on the burner and poured a cup. She sipped carefully to avoid further injury to her lip. Brand or no Brand. The liquid fortitude helped her face the day.

Looking around her small living room, she spotted

her large black bag. She recalled the gifts her friends gave her last night at the Pied Piper. Leaving her cup on the counter, she opened her purse and took out the white gift bag that Jules gave her. She slowly lifted out the pink tissue paper and unwrapped the leather biker babe teddy and whip. Uncoiling the whip, she slung it out, making it crack in the air.

"Wow."

She cracked it again as the front door opened, almost snapping Brand across the cheek.

"Whoa. Watch it." He flinched backward. "What was that?"

Carly hid the whip behind her. "What's what?"

Brand glared at her. "Don't play coy. You know what I'm talking about. That thing you're trying to hide behind your back. That thing that almost hit me in the face when I walked through the door."

She swallowed, reading his irritation loud and clear. He was a strong man. She didn't want to test him. "It's a whip."

"A whip? Why in the world do you have a whip? Is there something I should know about you? Are you into kink?"

"N-o-o! It was a gift."

"To ward off your ex-husband?"

Carly laughed, shaking her head. "Now that's a thought. But not what Jules had in mind when she purchased it."

"And exactly why would your friend buy you such a

thing?" He crossed his arms over his broad chest, making his biceps bulge.

"Because she wanted to bring out my hidden vixen?" Carly shrugged her shoulders and turned to go into the kitchen to put a little distance between the two of them. The conversation was getting a little too close for comfort.

The lock on the front door clicked while she busied herself with putting two pieces of bread in the toaster.

"Let me guess, the whip went with this?"

Carly froze. She didn't have to turn around to know that he'd found the biker babe leather teddy that she'd left by her purse.

She took a deep breath and decided to own up to the teddy. "That's right. It came in that very innocent looking virginal bag with pink tissue to boot."

Brand's chuckle made her relax. "So I take it your short shorts and studded boots last night wasn't your idea either?"

She slowly turned. "No. My friends bought that outfit for me to wear. They wanted me to live a little. To feel liberated from the confines of my marriage now that my divorce is final from Justin Porter. They thought I needed to go out and have a one-night stand to get over it all. But in the end, I came home ..."

"With me."

Her cheeks warmed and she went to the refrigerator, opening the door. She took out the small container of butter. Shutting the door back, she turned to face him. "Well, the evening didn't end the way any of us imagined. I had already decided I was going home alone with my treasures."

"Treasures. Plural? What else did you get? Or is it prying?"

She sighed and leaned forward against the counter. "Simone gave me leopard print handcuffs and Colleen gave me a gift bag of glow in the dark condoms. She is a safety girl."

He grinned, nodding his head. "I take it last night, going to the Pied Piper was outside your comfort zone?"

"Yeah. Everything about it was, but I went because I had been cut off from living since I married Justin Porter. Sure I did the country club scene for him. I had to keep up appearances to make him look good. He needed it for his job and his political aspirations. But I couldn't pursue a career. I couldn't have a baby, because it wouldn't fit in with his plans. I soon realized I didn't want to start a family with him. A child shouldn't be raised in a world like that."

The toaster dinged and she turned away, going to get the bread. She put it on a plate then she got a case knife to smear the butter. "Would you like some toast?" She finally looked at him when he didn't say anything in response to what she told him. He stood motionless, staring at her. She knew she'd said too much.

"How about some eggs to go with it?" Brand's voice startled her and she jumped. "You should get some protein in your system after drinking last night. How much did you drink, anyway?"

"Why does that matter?" she asked before biting into the toast.

"You still smell like tequila."

"I what?" She laid the toast on the plate and raised her arm, sniffing to see if she smelled anything on her skin. There was an unusual odor about her. "Oh, ugh. I'm going to go shower. Scrambled eggs with cheese."

Brand chuckled as Carly hurried from the room. Her reaction was adorable, but he knew he shouldn't have teased her about reeking of alcohol. It wasn't that bad. He'd been around guys who smelled worse. Hell, he'd been so drunk in the past, he couldn't put one foot in front of the other for twenty-four hours. It was a wonder his leader hadn't kicked his ass back to boot camp, but Rueger wasn't like that. He understood his men weren't perfect warriors. They were human and the toil of the job was going to get to them. Missions, victories as well as the many failed, haunted them like demons in the night. It was those times that drove them to drink more than they should. When that happened Rueger was tough but fair getting them back in line.

Brand poured himself the last of the coffee and set to make another pot. He sent a text to Donovan to check in with him, then one to McLeod. Finally, he sent one to Kincaid and waited to see which one was the first to respond. He also kept an ear tuned to the sound of the shower running. When it stopped he planned to begin working on the scrambled eggs for Carly and himself.

His phone pinged first from Donovan.

"Help! I'm being domesticated. She's got me doing her grocery shopping! "

Brand chuckled and typed his reply.

"Hey man. You wanted the redhead. Suck it up. Otherwise everything okay on your end?"

"Yeah. Sweet pad. Got my own room. What about you?"

"Sofa sleeper."

"Better than the floor."

"Do me a favor. Find out about Carly's ex-husband. I believe he's keeping tabs on her. I need to know what I'm dealing with over here."

"Will do. Over and out."

Brand began looking through the cabinets for a small fry pan and a bowl to crack the eggs into. He'd found the bowl when his phone pinged again. It was Kincaid.

"Still at hospital. Colleen lost consciousness in bus, hasn't woken yet. EMT thought it was shock. Doctor's concerned it's more. Will keep you posted."

"Oh man. Keep us posted."

He noticed the water was no longer running. It must have stopped while he was reading the text from Kincaid. Bending down, he looked in the drawer of the stove to see if the frypan was there. "Bingo."

Cracking eggs, he beat them with a fork. Turning the eye on, he put a small amount of butter in the pan to melt. Then he put some salt and pepper in the eggs and whisked them a few more times.

His phone pinged and he reached for it, seeing that McLeod had finally answered.

"With Jules at Youth Center."

"Youth Center?"

"Where she works. Had a meeting today. Lots of teens here."

"Anything of interest to report?"

"Not yet. Keeping eyes and ears open. Out."

Now that was interesting. Jules works at a youth center. He'd have to ask Carly more about that and see what he could learn from her to help Will out.

He poured the eggs in the pan and used the fork to move them around. He was careful not to scratch the bottom of the pan or to let the eggs stick. He dropped two more pieces of bread in the toaster. When Carly came out of her room dressed he was getting down another plate.

"That smells yummy."

"I hope it tastes that way." He took her cold toast, put it in the frypan, and returned the pan to the stove to warm it up. The side with the butter browned before he put it back on her plate. By then the toaster popped up his bread. He grabbed those, smeared butter on them, and laid them on his plate. Then he topped

Carly's coffee cup off with freshly brewed before refilling his own.

"Want some jelly?" she asked, opening the refrigerator up and pulling out a small jar of something pinkish red.

"What kind is it?"

"Peach butter. I got it at the farmers market."

"Sure."

She got out a spoon and opened the lid, scooping some onto her plate before handing the jar to him.

He caught a whiff of raspberries and wondered if that was a body spray or her shampoo. She'd changed into camel-colored twill pants and a light blue blouse with a rounded collar like his granny had worn when he was a kid. He glanced down, noticing the petite dress flats she wore. Her hair was styled, jewelry accessorized her outfit and her makeup was on as if she were going out. It made him feel bad that he couldn't let her leave the apartment. But who knew, perhaps this was the way she dressed to stay in, coming from a country club background. Didn't Hawkeye say that Porter was the country club type? And hadn't Carly said he'd wanted her to be his social butterfly? It would stand to reason Porter would have expected a certain style in her dress for every occasion. That behavior would be hard to break after so many years of conditioning.

"What's wrong?" she asked.

"Nothing."

"Are you sure? You keep staring at me. Did something happen to Colleen? You said last night that the EMTs were taking her to the hospital. Did you hear from your guy while I was showering?"

Brand let out a sigh. How had she jumped to that conclusion from him looking at her appearance?

"Settle down. I haven't heard anything bad about your friend. I did hear from Kincaid. They are still at the hospital. Your friend is resting and he was able to pull a few strings to keep her there until morning because of the shooting."

Boy was he stretching the truth and then some, but she was buying it word for word. He felt bad about that, but he didn't have any confirmed details to tell her yet. So it was best to keep her in the dark about what happened to Colleen at the Pied Piper.

"The jelly is good."

"Glad you like it. Why is Colleen at the hospital? I know they took her by ambulance last night to check her out, but why didn't they do it at the bar like they did everyone else?"

Brand took a gulp of his coffee. He should have known that question would come up today when she had more time to think about it. "I'm not an EMT, Carly."

"I want to go to the hospital and see her."

"You can't."

"Why not?"

"Because you can't leave the apartment until I've been given the clear that it's safe for you to go out."

"What? I can't leave? No. No. I have to be able to leave. I have a job interview next week. I have to go to that interview, Brand." She looked at him for a moment and then began pacing back and forth in the small kitchen area. She raised one hand. "I have to be able to support myself. This isn't fair. It isn't right." She stopped pacing and looked at him again, laying her hand on her chest. "I'm a victim here, but it sounds like I'm under house arrest while the bad guys are free to go wherever they please."

Brand reached out and took hold of her shoulders. "I will contact Commander Burns and see what I can do about you going to the job interview."

"And if he doesn't? What then? Who's going to pay my rent? The electric, water, and phone? Who's going to put food in my cabinets?"

"I get it." He released her shoulders. "Speaking of food. There isn't much in the cabinet or refrigerator right now. You make out a list of what you buy and I'll go do the shopping later today."

"I don't eat much. There's plenty."

He grinned. "That may be true, honey. But I'm a fella that likes his meat and vegetables. So while I'm here there's gonna be more than what's getting you by in this apartment. Don't worry about the cost either. I'm paying because I'm eating. So make out a list of what you want and I'll pick it up along with things I like. Also, point me in the direction of the closest place to go."

"I can afford to buy my own groceries."

"I didn't say you couldn't, but buying for two couldn't have been in your budget until you got a job."

She crossed her arms over her chest. "Fine. I'll make the list out. But I have coupons."

"I have no problem using those if that makes you happy."

A slow grin formed. "There's also a delivery service at the local grocery if you'd like to shop online. I haven't tried it here, but Justin Porter had me use it to free me up for his business."

Brand cocked his head to the side. "Why is it that every time you say the man's name it's always Justin Porter? Never plain Justin?"

"Because he is 'Justin Porter.'" She made air quotation marks when she said his name. "A frat buddy of his made the mistake of calling him only Justin on the eve of his wedding. He ended up getting married with a black eye. It isn't a mistake you want to make twice. It's a lesson you learn and remember ..."

"Okay. I get it." *Son of a bitch.* The man was a psychopath. Brand didn't want to know what Porter did to Carly if she'd called him Justin instead of Justin Porter.

"Want some more coffee?" he asked, trying to change the subject to something more pleasant.

"I'm good."

"What can you tell me about Jules and her job at the youth center?"

"Jules? Why?"

"I'm trying to get an understanding of all parties involved in what went down last night. The more you can tell me about your friends, the better I can understand the situation. You can trust me with the information you give me. Before I left the military, I had top security clearance. If I hadn't been deemed medically unfit for combat, I would still be serving my country on foreign soil instead of helping protect its citizens on the home front."

Carly nodded, took a deep breath and then let it out slowly. "She's a psychologist... a youth counselor and she really cares about the kids there. But she's really more than that. She's an advocate, going to bat for them to keep the programs and after-school activities. Funding to the center gets cut every time you turn around it seems. Like right now. That is all she has been dealing with this week. The center has lost a prestigious donor. Jules is terrified the center might close if this happens again."

"What about any of the youth at the center. Has Jules mentioned anyone in particular?"

"What do you mean? Like someone she sees has the potential to rise above his home life? If so, yeah, there is this one kid she's really afraid will fall into the gang life if the center closes. She's been working with him for years to keep it from happening, but he's just now reached the age when the pressure is on. That's why these cuts at the center are so hard on Jules. I'm sure your guy must think he's been assigned to a shrew, but she sees herself in this kid. She came from the wrong side of the tracks. Jules Gentry wouldn't be where she is today if it wasn't for the youth center in Brooklyn Heights or the counselor who made a difference in her life."

Brand swallowed. He took in every word that Carly said about her friend and her passion for the youth center. Even the kids there. "What's this kid's name that Jules has been so keen on?"

Carly shook her head, scrunching her eyes closed. "Sorry. I – I know she has talked about him, but if she ever said his name I don't recall. I've been focused so much on my divorce lately that minute details like that don't always stick with me."

"I get it. What you've told me is a good start. Maybe talking about it will jog your memory and his name will come to you when you least expect it. I'm not saying this kid has joined a gang yet. But a hit at a bar during closing hours like what happened last night does sound like an initiation ritual."

Carly opened her eyes and a tear escaped. "That would be horrible if it were true, Brand. But those boys did look older than any that visit the youth center."

She put the lid back on the peach butter, and then the lid on the small container of butter. Stacking them, she took both to the refrigerator. It was a clear sign she was finished eating and ready to move on with her morning routine. Even if Brand had more questions he wanted to be answered.

"What about Simone. What can you tell me that could help give me a good picture of her and why the gunman would single her out?"

"He was loony tunes. I've thought about it myself. Anyone who would point a gun at another human being for no reason and pull the trigger, then laugh like a lunatic. He laughed, then Phil's shooter laughed when he threatened to shoot me. Do you think they were high on something?"

"Possibly." Brand agreed with her, gathering their dishes and putting them in the sink. "Other than the shooter and what you think about him, I want you to think about your friend. Is there anything out of the ordinary in Simone's life? Anything odd that sticks out that could have caused someone to come after her? You don't have to answer right away if you need to think about it for a moment."

"She told you last night there wasn't, but I noticed she bit her bottom lip. I've found that's a tell-tale sign she's lying. I don't know about what, but there is something she wasn't saying. Whether it's about her, her job, or her fa—"

Brand watched Carly shut down. She rinsed the plates and stowed them in the small dishwasher to run later. He waited as she squirted dish liquid in the frypan and washed it, before rinsing and drying.

"Her what?" he prompted.

"Father. It seems I recall her saying something recently about not being able to reach him. She's left him several messages on his phone, but he hasn't returned them. Before she left town on her last business trip, she made the comment that she was concerned something was wrong, he wasn't at work. His secretary hadn't seen him in days, yet his business partners weren't concerned at all. That really had her upset."

"Is this normal for him?"

"Clayton Reid." Carly nodded. "He's a wheeler-dealer type. That's why Simone is as good a sales rep for her company, but she's honest to the core, while her dad has been known to do some shady deals in the past."

"Anything else about Simone?"

"Her parents divorced when she was young. Her mother remarried to a real-estate developer who adored Simone, so she had the best of both worlds. She had two men in her life who loved her but were from the opposite end of the spectrum in ethics."

"What about this stepfather?"

"Stanwell. Leland Stanwell. Gloria and Leland moved to Miami five years ago. He's semi-retired. Dabbles still in real-estate."

"So Jules is from the wrong side of the tracks. Simone's dad is shady. Stepfather is in real-estate.

These don't sound like friends of someone from a country club background."

Carly grinned. "We met in college. The place my father had no control over who I'd be around. Of course, you haven't asked me about Colleen. Her parents are divorced, yet they have remained friends. Joan and Bob Summers work in corporate offices in downtown Chicago. They do Saturday brunch with her almost every weekend. She came from the good side of town as I did."

"Thank you. I didn't ask about her because she didn't witness the shooting or the gang members like you, Jules or Simone. But it is nice to know how she fits into your little circle of friends."

"Speaking of Colleen…Can you call your friend Wyatt and see if he has an update on her? It would make me feel better knowing how she is."

Brand nodded. "I'll check in with him while you make out the shopping list."

"I've got paper and pen in my room. I'll give you some privacy."

## CHAPTER 5

BRAND WAITED until Carly was in her bedroom and closed the door before he texted Wyatt for an update on Colleen. He didn't expect to receive any news from him, but his phone pinged back immediately.

"She's awake. Doc with her now. Commander Burns located her parents. Bad mistake. Arguing over which one should take her home. Haven't told them she's not going with them."

"Take charge of the situation."

"Will do."

"Report back when you know more on Colleen's condition."

"Over and out."

Brand pulled out his note pad and jotted down important facts that Carly had told him. He would check them out later tonight after she was asleep so she wouldn't walk in on him. The last thing he needed was a million questions about what he was doing.

The bedroom door opened and she emerged with a list and several coupons for him to use. "Here is some cash towards the groceries. I know you said you'd get it, but I would feel better if you at least allowed me to chip in some on it. I've added a few personal items that I had planned to get when I went shopping anyway. Unless you'll allow me to go to the local drug store down the street to get these items myself?"

He took the stack she handed him and glanced at it, spotting a coupon for feminine products on top. He swallowed and tried not to grimace. Was she forcing him to buy the product out of need or in retaliation? Then he saw the mascara and powder compact shade #C058 on the list as well. Okay, maybe these were legit requests. After all, she did offer to go the local drugstore to get them herself if he'd let her. Which was out of the question.

Folding the money, list, and coupons, he stashed them in his front pocket. "No. I can get these for you with the other stuff. No problem at all."

She smiled. "Okay then. Is it a problem if I go down to the laundry room in the building while you're gone? Or would you prefer I wait until you return to go with me?"

"I'll go down with you and check the place out before I leave. If I feel it's safe for you to return alone, then you are free to move about in the building without concern."

"Fair enough," she said. "Do you really think someone would try to come after me?"

"If I can be candid with you?"

"Please."

"You did get a good look at the two gang members who got away and you prevented the shooter from escaping as well. That is enough to put you on their hit list to take you out."

"You don't mince words, Brand. I like that about you. I bet your team does as well."

He shrugged. "I get no complaints from them."

"Give me a moment to grab my laundry basket and I'll be ready to head down. If you have anything you want to wash while I'm down there, feel free to bring it along."

"You're assuming I'll give you the all clear."

"I like to keep a positive attitude. Besides, even if you don't, I can at least put my laundry in the wash and come back up until you return. If someone needs the washer, they'll take it out and put it in my basket for me to put in the dryer."

He grunted, finding it hard not to smirk at her reasoning. "Okay. If you don't mind my throwing in some dirty laundry, I'll take you up on that offer."

While she left, he grabbed his duffle to take down.

CARLY DIDN'T WAIT for Brand to give the all-clear before she threw her load in the washer. She had it started before he shoved his clothes in two empty washers and they headed back upstairs. "Looks like you really needed to do laundry."

"We were here all week and headed to the airport when we were reassigned to watch over you girls …er, women last night."

"So is it okay for me to go back down in thirty to check on the clothes?"

He nodded. "For a basement laundry room, it is well lit. The elevator is in great working order and the lighting in the stairwell is excellent as well. You have options on which way you travel if one path makes you feel safer over the other. Don't get spooked, but keep your eyes and ears open at all times. Do you have a neighbor in the building that you have gotten to know since you moved in? Maybe you could go down together?"

"Afraid not. I haven't lived here that long."

"It was worth a shot. Okay. I'll leave you to go back to your apartment and I'll go get the groceries. I'll be back soon."

Carly started to wave but stopped. "Did you by chance hear from Kincaid about Colleen?"

"She's awake. A doctor was in with her, but her parents are there arguing over who should take her home with them."

Carly shook her head. "That's the last thing she needs. Thanks for the update. See you."

She hurried up the flights of stairs to her apartment and called Simone.

"Hey, good to hear your voice. Are you alone?" Simone asked.

"Yes. Are you?"

"I am. Sent my guy out shopping. What did you do?"

"Same. Or rather, he insisted. The reason I called is I got info on Colleen. She's still at the hospital. Brand said it was because she was resting last night. I have a funny feeling something more is going on than he is telling me. He also said she's awake and that the doctor was checking her out. But, her parents are there arguing over which one is going to take her home. That makes me believe something happened last night that we don't know about. Don't you agree? Otherwise, why would they be arguing over her going home with one of them?"

"You always have a sixth sense, Carly, except when it came to Justin Porter. If you have a feeling something isn't right with Colleen, I believe you. We should go to the hospital and see her."

"I don't know. It's too risky. Brand said our lives are in danger."

"Are you sure you can trust him completely? Especially if he is keeping secrets about Colleen from us."

"Maybe he is telling me all he can when he can. Besides, he found a man watching the place last night.

63

The man was still here this morning and he found out the guy works for Justin Porter."

"What! I'm coming over. You don't need to be left alone if that slime ball Porter has a man following you."

"What about your safety, Simone?" Carly asked. "I don't want you putting your life in jeopardy on my account. You've already had a gun pointed at you and the trigger pulled."

"Don't you worry your pretty little head over that. Donnie and I had a long discussion about it this morning and we agree it was a fluke."

"Donnie?"

"Donovan. My guy. He said he got the nickname Don Juan from his Marine buddies. But until I see him put the moves on me and he earns those stripes, I'm going to refer to him as Donnie."

"Simone, be real. He's not going to put the moves on you. He's here to protect you. Not seduce you."

"No man alive can resist me when I make a play for him. You watch. I'll have little Donnie in my hands before the week's out."

"Little Donnie. I don't even want to know what you mean by that."

"You already do, Carly. So tell me, when are you going to put my handcuffs to work?"

"None of your business. I don't kiss and tell."

"Isn't that the truth! You're no fun in the bedroom." Simone took a breath. "I've got confirmation from my

Uber on pickup. I'll be there soon and call when I'm outside your building."

"You shouldn't be doing this."

"Be ready when I get there. We're going to see Colleen."

The phone line went dead before Carly could protest further. She went to her bedroom closet, got a basket out of the bottom and headed back to the laundry room. She left it on the washers Brand was using so if anyone came down while she was gone, they'd put the clothes in it. She knew Brand would be pissed when he came back and found her gone. If she couldn't talk Simone out of her plan to go to the hospital, she'd be going along with her. At least the two of them wouldn't be traveling alone.

Carly and Simone got out of the Uber at the entrance to Chicago Med and went inside to the information desk. They typed in Colleen's name at the kiosk to find out what floor she was on before heading to the bank of elevators.

Once inside the elevator, Carly turned to Simone. "I still think this was a bad idea."

"You didn't have to come with me," Simone pointed out. "You could have stayed at your apartment doing your laundry."

"No, I couldn't. I'd have worried the whole time that you were in danger. The smart thing was for you to stay at your place until Donovan returned."

"Live a little, Carly. Take chances."

The elevator dinged, signaling they'd arrived on their floor. The doors opened and the girls stepped out. All discussion about what was right or wrong ceased. They followed the corridor signs down the hallway to Colleen's room.

The sound of arguing voices wafted down the hall and the two looked at one another.

"Geeze, I hope they aren't in her room doing that."

"Mr. and Mrs. Summers never had tact when it came to disagreeing," Simone said.

Someone made a sharp pitched whistle sound cutting them off. "Enough. I know you want what's best for your daughter, but this isn't it." A door shut, ending them overhearing whatever was being said on the matter.

"Was that Colleen's guy?" Carly asked.

"Sounded like it. We better hurry and find her while he's preoccupied with mom and dad or we're busted."

"Oh, now you think of that."

Simone rolled her eyes. She grabbed Carly's arm, dragging her with her down the hall at a faster pace toward the nurses' station.

Colleen's room was across the hall from the station, which was good. The nurses could watch who went in and out at all times. They went inside and slid the curtain back so no one would see them visiting with her.

"Oh my God," Simone gasped when she saw the

bruising and swelling on Colleen's face. Carly focused in on the busted lip.

"She must have been attacked in the bathroom. That's the reason she was in there so long," Carly said. "And you wanted to leave when those guys came in."

"I-I had no idea. The three of us had been to that bar so many times before. It was always a safe place to go until last night. Do you think she was raped?" Simone whispered.

Carly moved to the opposite side of the bed and reached for Colleen's hand that didn't have an IV sticking in it. Sweet Colleen.

Her friend flinched at her touch. Her eyes fluttered opened and her lips began to tremble once she focused. Tears began to roll down her cheeks.

"Sh-h-h, don't cry. It's okay. You're okay. You're safe." Carly patted her hand.

Simone stepped forward and brushed the hair away from Colleen's forehead. "We're here for you."

"What happened to me?" Colleen asked.

"You don't know?"

Colleen shook her head.

Carly looked at Simone, then back down at Colleen. "Honey, we don't know. Do you remember going out with us on Friday night?"

"Yes. I remember dancing with you guys, but that is it."

"We were getting ready to leave, but you had to go to the restroom," Simone said. "So you went alone."

"We waited for you out front, at the bar, but then the bar got robbed. The bartender was shot and we were lucky to have gotten out alive. In all the chaos, we never knew what happened to you. We found out you were taken to the hospital last night to be checked out."

"Your parents are here, down the hall arguing about who's going to take you home. Have you seen them yet?" Simone asked.

Colleen groaned. "Carly, I know I made fun of your apartment last night, but let me go home with you."

They laughed.

"Hey, you're remembering something from last night. That is good." Carly smiled at her. "What did the doctor say when he saw you this morning?"

"That I needed to rest and stay here another day because of my memory loss and some tests they want to run on me."

"Did they examine you?" Simone asked.

Colleen nodded. "I wasn't... That didn't happen. For what did, I still feel violated. I don't remember it, but it feels like something horrible happened. My body feels icky and I want to shower a dozen times. I know I never want to wear that skirt again."

The curtain scrapped back fast and a younger, blonder version of Brand came into the room. Carly assumed this was Wyatt Kincaid and they were caught.

"Ladies, I don't assume you were given permission to be here?"

"Are you going to do something about it?" Simone

asked, walking toward him. She came nose to nose with him.

The guy didn't say a word, he slid the glass room door shut, pulled out his phone and punched in a number. Then he put the phone up to his ear. "Don Juan, I think you've lost something very important. You need to come to collect it now before I report you to Brand for slacking on your duties. It has red-hair and curvaceous ..."

The guy laughed into the phone. "See you then."

"Who's he?" Colleen asked.

"He's your protector," Carly explained. "We've all got a guy assigned to protect us after what happened last night at the bar."

"Really? Why?"

"The bar shooting was gang-related. Simone and I are witnesses inside. Jules saw the getaway car outside because she came back when she heard the gunshots."

"I heard them too."

"You did?"

Colleen nodded, closing her eyes. "That's what caused my attacker to run away."

Wyatt came over to the bed. "Did she say what I think she said?"

Carly nodded.

"Colleen, what else do remember from last night?" he asked.

"I'm tired. I need to rest now."

Wyatt punched in a few more numbers on his

phone and walked back toward the sliding doors. "Brand, Wyatt here. You need to come to Chicago Med. There's been a development. Sure. Get here as fast as you can. Thanks."

He turned around and looked at them. "Ladies, you might as well take a seat and get comfortable. You're gonna be here a while. And then you won't be able to sit without remembering the chewing out you get."

## CHAPTER 6

Brand hurried with the groceries to Carly's apartment. He expected to drop them off with her before heading to Chicago Med to check-in with Wyatt. Yet, he found the place empty. A note card on the kitchen counter explained Simone had picked her up in an Uber and they had gone to see Colleen.

"Dammit to hell."

Why hadn't Wyatt said that was the reason he needed him at the hospital?

He shoved the cold and freezer items into the refrigerator and left the rest. He headed back downstairs to catch a taxi to the hospital. The nearest "L" line was five blocks away, and he'd get to the hospital quicker this if there wasn't a traffic jam.

He tried not to think about that as he waited to hail a taxi. All he wanted to think about was getting to the hospital and Carly before something happened to her.

Had it been a wrong move on his part to trust her to stay at her apartment while he ran to the grocery? He hadn't thought so at the time, but now he was beginning to think otherwise. He thought he had made it clear the danger she could be in if she wasn't careful.

A taxi pulled up and he jumped in, giving his destination to the driver. He was certain he'd gotten his point across to Carly before he left. The blame for her going against his wishes had to lie with Simone and Donovan not doing his job. He wouldn't jump to any conclusions until he assessed the situation further. After he talked to Donovan and Kincaid.

Fifteen minutes later Brand entered the hospital and ran into Hawkeye at a bank of elevators.

"I wasn't expecting you to be here checking up on your man," Hawkeye said.

"He called and said he needed my help."

"You felt confident enough to leave your charge alone in her apartment?"

"Not exactly."

Hawkeye's brow arched as the elevator dinged and a set of doors opened. The men got on and rode up in silence, though Brand could feel Hawkeye watching him. The doors opened again and they got off, walking down the hallway.

"What do you mean, not exactly?"

"I left her alone to do some shopping, but she didn't stay. I've come here to retrieve her."

Hawkeye's chuckle reverberated up and down the

hallway. He slapped Brand on the back. "Not exactly indeed."

Donovan ran into them before the nurses' station, coming from the opposite direction. "Wyatt called you both in about this? I swear I only left Simone alone to go get a few groceries and some things she declared she had to have. I never imagined she'd leave her apartment."

"So it happened to both of you?" Hawkeye said.

Brand grimaced.

"Both of us?" Donovan looked at Brand.

"Yeah, both Carly and Simone are here visiting Colleen. I guess Wyatt didn't tell you that?"

"No. He told me I lost something and if I didn't want him telling you, I'd better get here fast."

Hawkeye chuckled.

"This isn't funny," Brand grumbled.

"Not at all," Donovan agreed.

"I beg to differ. Two females giving highly trained military operatives the slip. You can fight for this country, are trained to serve and protect, yet you can't keep them in their apartments? This isn't going to look good when I try to get funding for a program going here in Chicago if you can't even keep these two safe."

"It won't happen again," Brand assured him.

"It better not. I'm counting on all four of you to do your jobs and make my task easy. I want this program for my city."

"We understand," Brand said. "Don't we, Donovan?"

"Yes, Sir. We have your six on this."

The sliding glass door to a room across from the nurses' station opened and Wyatt came out, closing the door back. "I thought I heard voices. Before you go in there chewing the girls out, their visit has been good for Colleen. She's been responsive. She has even remembered things about last night with them that my questioning couldn't get her to recall. I know they disobeyed and risked their lives coming here, but it has turned out good in the end. I still would bring the wrath of God down on them, but keep in mind what good was accomplished."

"Did she get a good look at her attacker? Should we bring down a sketch artist?" Hawkeye asked.

"She hasn't proclaimed that yet, but she did say she heard the gunshots and that is why her attacker ran off. She has napped. When she woke she talked of her attacker taking her purse. She's afraid of her credit cards getting maxed out. She's also concerned about her apartment and getting robbed. That's the reason I contacted your office, Commander."

"I was in the area so I dropped by to see how things were going."

"How did her parents take the news she wasn't going home with them?" Brand asked.

"Not well. When I explained she wasn't going to her apartment, but a safe house, they agreed. In return, I promised to keep them well aware of what was going on with her."

"You handled that well, Kincaid." Hawkeye stepped forward and touched him on the shoulder. "Let's go in and meet this courageous young woman and her daring friends under better circumstances."

Brand grunted. Better? He didn't call this better. It was a different mess than the one they'd been in the night before. He was ready to stop meeting under these circumstances. He was glad to hear that Colleen had responded to Carly's visit for Wyatt's sake. But, it didn't change the fact that she had left the safety of her apartment to come to the hospital. If she thought he was going to bat for her now so she could go on that job interview next week, she had another think coming. She'd have to forgo it and start looking for another job after her protection detail was over. He couldn't risk having her out there and something happen to her. It wasn't just the gang retaliating that he had to worry about, but her ex-husband Justin Porter. He didn't have a clue what that deranged asshole might try.

He noticed a chill in the room as soon as the curtain was pushed aside. He spotted Carly and Simone sitting in straight back chairs across the room. Colleen turned her head toward the doorway.

"This is Commander Burns from Chicago PD, Brand Chambers, and Liam Donovan," Wyatt explained. "They are here to check in on how things are going and to collect Simone and Carly."

"What if we don't want to go?" Simone asked, sounding defiant.

Brand noticed a tick in Hawkeye's jaw, a clear sign he'd picked up on her tone as well.

"You'll do what you're told, young woman or I'll have you taken down to central booking," Hawkeye told her.

"On what charges?" she challenged.

"Impeding an investigation."

"And how would I be doing that?"

"By causing more work for your protector and the police to make sure you're safe. My officers need to be out in the field looking for your friend's attacker, not to mention the gang members who tried to rob the Pied Piper. I'm sure I could come up with other charges to keep you in a holding cell until we find the perps if it means keeping you safe. Or you can go back to your apartment with Mr. Donovan and stay in comfort. Is that enough reason for you to see you should be in your apartment where it is safe?"

"I do have to go back to work Monday."

"Then he'll go with you. I'll send a driver and a car around for your use."

"I have a job interview next week. I need this job to pay my bills. Please, can I keep the interview?" Carly asked.

"No. Not after this stunt," Brand barked.

"Brand, take it down a notch." Hawkeye arched a brow at him, before turning toward Carly. "I don't see why that should be a problem if Brand goes with you. We want you to carry on your normal routine as much as possible. The two of you aren't under house arrest by any means. But, we do want to keep you both safe and we're trying to take measures to ensure that. If it feels like your wings of freedom are clipped short-term, that's all it is—a temporary situation. Can you both understand that? Coming here today was a risk neither of you should have taken."

"Thank you, Commander." Carly swallowed. "There is one more thing. I'd like to be able to go to the bartender's funeral whenever that is to pay my respects to his wife if possible. Can that be arranged?"

The Commander was hesitant for a moment, but he finally nodded. "That can happen, Ms. Manning. I'm sure his wife will appreciate that."

Carly liked this Commander Burns. He explained things a little better than Brand did, but she got where Brand was coming from as well. She understood he was there to protect her and he wanted to make sure she was safe. She knew she had done wrong by coming with Simone to the hospital to see Colleen, but she'd come along anyway. She'd made the choice and she would suffer the consequences for it when she was alone with Brand. That's the reason she'd asked about the job interview when Simone mentioned going to work. If her friend could go to her day job, then Carly felt she should be able to go on a job interview. She needed this job. She had bills coming due and no way to pay them. What savings she had while married to Justin Porter paid for the divorce and now she had to have a paycheck.

Simone leaned toward her. "Geeze your guy is a hard ass."

"He's tough, but fair."

"You're not defending him are you?"

Carly half-shrugged. "I get him."

"You and the men you pick."

"I haven't picked him."

Simone tilted her head and looked at her hard. "If you say so."

She shook her head, knowing it was better not to argue with Simone over this point and let it slide. Instead, she went back over to hold Colleen's hand while the commander asked her a few questions.

"I-I'm not sure what he looked like. He came through the door so fast and hit me in the face with his hand. I-I don't think I'd be any help for a sketch artist."

"You may think that now, but I'd like you to try. We can bring in a behavioral scientist who can take you on a journey through a series of questions. The results will help you reveal more than you ever imagined you'd remember."

"Like a profiler?" Colleen asked. "Something like they do on *Criminal Minds*?"

The commander nodded. "But this method is real."

"How soon can you have someone here?" Wyatt asked.

"I can arrange to get someone here as early as this afternoon. The sooner we can get a sketch of her attacker, the better we'll be able to find him."

"When do you think Colleen will be released from the hospital?" Carly ventured to ask.

"That is up to the doctor," Wyatt said. "He wasn't hopeful this morning but that was because he wanted to run tests."

"So her staying here has nothing to do with trying to keep her in a safe location?" Carly questioned.

"If that was what we were going for, we'd have to have a guard posted outside her door to track who comes in and out of this room. A hospital is too public to be safe." The commander turned to Brand. "My car and driver are downstairs. You and Donovan can escort the women to their respective apartments for now. I'll order a car detail for you both to have at your disposal. All you have to do is call when you want it. I'll send both of you the information."

"Thanks, Hawkeye." Brand motioned to Carly. "Say your good-byes so we can head out."

She nodded and looked down at Colleen, giving her hand a squeeze. "I'll see you soon. I know you're in good hands with Wyatt. You can call me if you want to talk."

"Good luck on your interview."

"Thanks. I'll need it." Carly stepped away from the bed and turned toward Simone. "Let's go girl."

"You're going to let him order you around like that?" Simone questioned.

"He's not ordering me around. It's time to go. Colleen needs to rest. Can't you see how tired she looks?"

"Simone!" Donovan said, his tone full of irritation.

Carly watched her friend's head snap in his direction. There was also a knowing look in Simone's eye. A tell-tale sign that all her talk was bluster and that Donovan was the real one in charge in her apartment.

"Yes, Donnie?" the words purred from her mouth.

Brand grunted. "Donnie?"

Carly pivoted in time to see Donovan look at Brand and shake his head. He said something to Brand that Carly couldn't make out from across the room.

Simone sidled up to her and whispered in her ear. "I got him right where I want him. Before the week's out. I tell you before the week is out."

Carly rolled her eyes and tried to stifle a laugh. She felt sorry for Donovan for having to deal with her friend if Simone did put the moves on him.

## CHAPTER 7

THE DRIVE to the respective apartment buildings was quiet. Brand sat up front while Donovan sat in the middle row of the SUV with Carly and Simone. He couldn't get over Carly going to see Colleen after he'd explained the dangers of her leaving the apartment. What had made her think she could disregard him? He heard a slight giggle out of Simone, answering his question. Yeah, Simone is what happened. He knew from the moment he'd met the redhead that she was reckless.

It wasn't like he could further limit Carly's contact with her friend. They lived in different apartment buildings. Their only contact was through phone calls and he couldn't prohibit that. He'd come across as heartless. And he didn't want Carly to resent him or not trust him. That would work against his protecting her.

He hadn't been on many assignments like this since being back in the states. Most of his assignments working for Hank Patterson had dealt with corporate America. He'd seen the way Hawkeye looked at him when he put his foot down about Carly going on the interview. He could have handled that with more finesse. He definitely should have handled it better. The woman had lived with an asshole for seven years and here he was acting like a brute. He already knew she needed a job to pay her bills, but dammit, she'd risked her life needlessly. But, it had not been the best move on his part.

He looked out the window, watching as the SUV traveled along the crowded streets to the suburban area. It reminded him of the neighborhood where he'd grown up in Dallas. High and low rises on both sides of the streets, little green space on either side. That was a messed up time in his life when he ran with the wrong crowd and was in trouble more than he was not. He'd ended up dropping out of college, but thank God the military had straightened him out. The SEALs had given his life focus, purpose–until one career ending bullet to the chest.

Damn. He hated how his thoughts always went back to that time in Afghanistan. How he'd had to leave the SEALS over one fatal mistake his partner Joe made. That's why he didn't want to see Carly make a bad judgment call. She didn't need to end up dead over something that might seem as trivial as not packing a tactical bag right.

The driver slowed the SUV to a stop in front of Carly's apartment building and they got out, saying their good-byes.

Brand did a quick sweep of the area with his eyes and frowned. "I see we have surveillance still."

"We do?" Carly stepped toward him.

"Yeah. Apparently, my warning did nothing to deter Ragsdale this morning. So let's give your ex something to think about." Brand wrapped a protective arm around her shoulders and pulled her to him. He dipped his head as if he were planting a kiss on the top of hers and inhaled the raspberry scent after she showered. He was ready to set her away before he forgot this was an assignment and he was still annoyed with her.

She wrapped her arm around his waist, reinforcing their contact until they walked through the front doors. It wasn't until they were well inside away from the doorway that they broke apart.

"I know you're upset over my going to the hospital. I knew I shouldn't have gone, but Simone was going regardless and I couldn't let her do it alone. I remembered you wanted me to have someone go down to the laundry room with me, so I knew you'd prefer we traveled in pairs."

He took in a slow breath, seeing how she was twisting his words to defend her actions. "This isn't the place to have this discussion. We'll talk about it in your apartment. First, we need to collect our laundry. It should be dry by now, right?"

Carly shook her head. "I left before I put it in the dryers."

"Then we need to take care of it before we do anything else."

They took the stairs down to the laundry room and found their wet clothes waiting for them in the baskets sitting on the machines. Brand tossed him in the dryer. Carly sorted her clothes, putting some of the items into a dryer and taking the others upstairs to hang to dry. Then they went upstairs. Carly went to her room and hung what needed to hang while Brand started trying to sort the remaining groceries that needed putting away. When she finished she came to the kitchen to help him.

"When I said it was better to go down to the laundry room with someone, I wasn't saying it was safer for you to leave the apartment with someone other than me. I think you really knew that before you got in that Uber with Simone. Didn't you?"

Carly held a few cans of vegetables in her hands, nodded, and then put them in the five-shelf pantry unit. "I won't do it again."

"Don't tell me that because you think that is what I want to hear if you aren't going to do it."

"I wouldn't do that."

"I didn't think you'd leave the apartment today either, but you did."

She looked at him for a moment. "That's fair. I never should have called Simone. If I hadn't we wouldn't have gone to see Colleen. The blame lies on me. Sure she was the one who insisted on coming over even after I tried to talk her out of it. She was dead set we were going to see Colleen."

"Does Simone Uber often?" he asked.

"Sure. Most people in the city do. I haven't, but now that I don't have a car I might if I need to get somewhere instead of using a taxi."

"Why don't you have a car?" he asked before thinking.

"It was in Justin Porter's name. I didn't realize it all these years, but that came out in the divorce division of assets." Carly continued putting cans and boxes of food in the cabinet as she talked. "I thought I had contributed so much to the marriage. I walked away with my clothes and jewelry and a private bank account. I kept that hidden from Justin Porter because Jules set it up for me as a subaccount at her bank."

"That was smart of her. I'm glad to hear it." Brand picked up the bags on the floor and looked through them, before wadding them up and stuffing them into one. "I think that has got it all."

Carly frowned and looked around the kitchen for a moment. "No. I don't think so. What about the personal items I asked you to pick up?"

"I put that bag in the bathroom for you to go through."

"Oh. That makes sense. Thanks and thank you for picking them up for me." She turned, heading toward her room.

"Carly, what do you do on a Saturday?"

She stopped. "Laundry, groceries, clean the apartment, read a good book, or get together with my friends. It's getting warmer weather. We sometimes go to the park or find a café where we can have a late lunch or early dinner and sit on the patio and talk. Why?"

"What do you want to do today?"

She took a deep breath. "Well. There isn't much to do around here today because I cleaned yesterday. I had only one small load of laundry left to do today. If you want to get out of here this afternoon, only the residents know about a rooftop garden spot. We could take our food up there and eat."

He nodded. "Do you like movies?"

"Of course. Who doesn't?" She grinned. "I like action-adventure, comedy, drama, as well as the chick-flicks guys hate. So if you want to rent something or check out what's free over the internet via Amazon or Netflix, I'll show you how to log in."

"Okay. We can do that later." He nodded. "And dinner on the roof sounds good too. I could sear a couple of steaks for us."

"Steaks?"

"Oh yeah. I got steaks today. There was this mark-down section in the meat department. I was browsing when the meat counter employee came out with a tray of marked down packages of cuts. I couldn't believe the choice pieces. I put a few in your freezer, but left a pack in the fridge for later."

She grinned. "You don't shop much do you?"

His enthusiasm slowly faded. "This wasn't a surprise to you, was it?"

"No. Smart shoppers look for bargains like the quick sale markdown section in the meat department. Just like clipping coupons and signing up for stores' reward cards to get additional discounts. And even shopping more than one store to get weekly sales."

"In the military, you have the PX."

"And what about since you've been out?"

"I've been in Eagle Rock, Montana, and it's a small town. Shopping is limited. Usually, if I want steak, I find out when Cookie is grilling them up at the Brighter Days Rehab Ranch and pop in there for a home cooked meal."

"Cookie?"

"Carl Fite. He's the cook over there. Brighter Days is a rehabilitation ranch for ex-military who need extra help recuperating. Sometimes they need help dealing after leaving Walter Reed or other military hospitals. It also is a rehabilitation ranch for horses. Some come there because humans have physically abused them. Others have been starved nearly to death and would otherwise be euthanized. Sometimes the horses are homeless because their owners die. The purpose of the ranch is to give ex-military men and women who are coping with their own shortcomings because of injuries in combat a new meaning in life while helping these animals. It's a great program. As a PTSD patient, Wyatt spent time there adjusting to life and learning to work with his service dog, Ruby. That is why Hawkeye, I mean, Commander Burns, assigned him to your friend Colleen. The trauma of the attack will leave her with similar PTSD symptoms that Wyatt can help her deal with in the next several weeks."

"Hawkeye? … Was Commander Burns former military?" Carly asked.

Brand nodded. "Former SEAL. He wasn't DEVGRU like me, but he went through the same training unit class as I did. In the end, we got assigned to different areas."

"DEV—"

"DEVGRU. It's the elite of the SEALS. You don't hear talk about us much. We're deep six because we have more clearance than other SEALS. I'm telling you this because I want you to understand that I have the power to protect you in every way possible, Carly. If the gang comes after you physically, I can take them out with my body. If they try to come after you through hacking into your computer or electronics, I've got the skill set to stop them. Even if it isn't the gang doing it, but your ex-husband doing it, I will take him down. I'm your man, Carly."

She swallowed, looking overloaded by all he told

her. "Thank you for your service, Brand, and for what you are willing to do for me. I had better go get my basket. The clothes should be ready for us to get out of the dryer."

"Okay."

While she was gone, he wondered if he'd told her too much, but dismissed the thought. She needed to know he could protect her no matter what. He believed she was more afraid of what Justin Porter might do than the gang members would attempt and that really pissed him off. It should be the other way around. Justin wouldn't get his hands dirty trying to kill her, but the gang member wouldn't think twice about putting a bullet in her head. But how could he make her see that without coming across as a brute?

Carly came out and they went down to the laundry room. They retrieved the dry clothes, folded and put them in the basket before returning upstairs. She was very quiet, not saying more than a few words to him the whole time. He figured she was still thinking about what he'd said. She was headed to her room when she stopped and turned to him.

"I have a drawer I can empty for you to put your things in and anything that needs to hang, I will be happy to make room in the closet for you," Carly offered.

He hesitated before he accepted the offer. "Thanks. I guess that would be better than my duffle bag lying in your living room with clothes in it."

He grabbed the bag from the floor and followed her into her bedroom. Setting his basket and bag on her bed, he walked over to the window and looked out, seeing that Ragsdale was still sitting in his car, watching the place. He made a throaty growl sound.

Carly giggled. "What is it?"

"That P.I. is still down there. I told him this morning to get lost or I'd call the cops. He left, but as you saw when we returned, he was back and he hasn't left."

"So what. Let Justin Porter waste his money on some private dick watching my apartment building; let him get his thrills. I'm not going to worry about it. What can he do to me when I've got you, right?"

Brand slowly grinned at her words and the new-found confidence he heard in her voice. "Right."

"Okay. I've cleared out this drawer for you. What you can't get in here, we'll just hang. I have more room in the closet anyway. I took most of my swankier clothes to consignment when we first separated."

"Why didn't you take what you're wearing today?" he asked before he thought.

"What did you say?" She looked at him and then at herself in the mirror. "What's wrong with what I'm wearing?"

"That blouse looks like something my granny used to wear."

"It does?"

He nodded.

"Well. My mom bought it for me. The last thing she gave me before things went sour between us. I guess I chose to wear it today because I needed her near me right now, but I can't reach out to her."

"Sorry."

"No. You're right. It does make me look like a schoolmarm or something." Carly walked to her closet and swung open the doors. She immediately began sorting through the clothes, taking one top after another out and putting it back in before she settled on one. Then she pushed her clothes to one side of the closet to make room for his clothes. "There should be plenty of hangers in there for you. If not, we'll…uh… you can go get some."

Without another word, she went into the bathroom and shut the door. She was torn by what he'd said about the blouse and her appearance. He felt like an ass for bringing it up, but it had slipped out when she talked about taking clothes to the consignment store. He should have kept his mouth shut.

He hurried and hung his things in the closet and put the clothes in the drawer she had cleared for him before leaving the duffle in the stacked laundry baskets on the bottom of the closet floor. He closed the closet doors, then went back to the living room. It was almost four so he took out the package of steaks from the fridge and washed his hands before beginning to prepare dinner.

Carly was wearing a pair of leggings with the top

she changed into when she emerged from her bedroom. She'd changed her hairstyle and jewelry as well.

"Do you want a salad with the steaks?" Brand asked.

"Do you?"

"If you do."

She sighed. "I'd be just as happy with green beans, garlic mashed potatoes, and a hot roll."

"Then fix that."

In a flash, she had a pot out of the cabinet and on the stove. After slicing off two pats of butter to melt, she opened and drained most of the liquid off a mason jar of green beans. Then she added them to the pot. She ran water into a large glass measuring bowl and stuck it into the microwave for five minutes. Turning on the oven, she got out a round pan that she put four Hawaiian rolls in and stuck it in to warm as the oven heated.

"How much longer until the steaks are done?" she asked.

"Depends on how you like yours?"

"Medium well."

"Two minutes more on each side."

"Perfect."

When the microwave dinged, she got the measuring bowl out. She dumped in a package of instant garlic potatoes, stirring. "Do you like cheese in your potatoes and sour cream?"

"Sure."

She got both from the fridge and added them to the potatoes. Then she turned off the oven and removed the rolls. Finally, she stirred the green beans and turned the eye off as well. "I think we are ready to eat if your steaks are done."

He stood back in amazement. "Is this how you always cook?"

She shook her head. "Since my divorce, I've learned I can cut corners and still eat the way I like without all the work."

Taking down dinner plates, Brand noticed they didn't match, but he didn't say a word.

"I got these at a tag sale down the street for a quarter each. Can you believe that?"

"That's great. I don't see a nick or chip."

"Right. They were odds and ends that belonged to the woman's aunt who had passed. I didn't care. I needed something to eat off of and since I couldn't take anything from the house when I left, these would do nicely."

"The small plates we used this morning matched."

"Yep. I was lucky there. She had a set of four of those for fifty cents."

"Carly, I hear the pride in your voice for being able to furnish your place with these dishes so cheaply, but your story is making my stomach clench because I want to go over to your old address and beat that SOB piece of shit within an inch of his life for treating you the way he did."

He saw the glistening of moisture in her eyes right before she set the plates on the counter and hugged him. The action was unexpected. It stunned him for a split second, but then he wrapped his arms around her and held her for a moment.

"Thank you, Brand. You don't know what it means to me to hear another man say that. If I could have had my own father stand up for me when I was going through the divorce, it would have meant the world to me, but he wasn't there for me. He was on Justin Porter's side. Both my parents were. I've been so alone in this other than Jules, Simone, and Colleen. If it wasn't for them, I don't know where I would have been."

Holding her against his chest felt nice and his anger at Porter subsided a little. He focused the emotion back on Carly and taking care of her needs and protecting her. He knew he should say something, but what. *Your parents should have their asses kicked for turning their backs on you.* That wasn't comforting.

"I'd never treat my own daughter that way."

Carly broke their embrace and stepped away from him. "Do you have a wife and a daughter?"

He shook his head. "No. I'm single. Never married. No children. I was speaking figuratively."

"Then you don't know how you'd handle a situation like this. In a different set of circumstances, you might feel differently."

"No." His voice was strong when he spoke. "I don't

think I'd ever side with anyone other than my own flesh and blood. No matter what the circumstances."

She smiled. "You're a good man, Brand. Rough around the edges. Blunt to a fault. But a good man. We better eat before the food gets cold. You still want to go up on the roof?"

He nodded thinking about what she'd just said. *Rough around the edges. Blunt to a fault. But a good man.*

CARLY SAT BACK on the cushioned bench, sipping her tea, and watched Brand finish his food. "Do you want me to run back down and get more food for you?" she asked.

He shook his head. "I'm good."

"That was a good steak. What did you put on it? More than salt and pepper. Did I taste garlic?"

"Yes, but it was hard to tell with the garlic mashed potatoes."

She stacked the empty dishes. "Would you like to take a walk and see the garden spot fully?"

He stood. "Are there table and benches at every large planter box like this one?"

"No. There are only two more up here like that. Then there is the fire pit in the center with chairs around it."

"Clearly I was wrong about this being just a respectable hole in the wall place to live."

Carly giggled. "No, you're right. The residents before me got together and made this a place to come to make it worth living here. Local businesses donated materials and one of the tenants is a carpenter, so he made the planter boxes, benches, the chairs, and tables. Another tenant works at a greenery and he got a deal on the trees, shrubs and flowering plants."

"The owner of the building didn't object?"

"He was all for it. It has brought more tenants to the building because of this spot."

"A win-win then without the owner having to fork over a penny."

"But you are wrong there. The owner did chip in on the plants and the décor. There is even covers for the furnishings to protect from the elements I'm told."

"I stand corrected."

Carly reached for his hand and led him over to her favorite reading spot, a bamboo oversized cushioned chair with an umbrella stand beside it. "Sometimes it is good just to come up here and hang out instead of going out."

"Like we're doing."

"Exactly."

A couple teens came out the roof door with a radio. The door opened again and a few more teens appeared carrying food and drinks. Carly dropped his hand. "Looks like they're going to have a party. Maybe we should go back downstairs."

"Sure. Whatever you say."

They got their dishes and went back downstairs to the apartment. Carly unlocked the door. "I'll clean up."

"I don't mind helping."

"You cooked and did the dishes this morning. Plus, you did the shopping. I'll do tonight."

"Okay. I'll grab a shower then."

"Towels and wash cloths are in the cabinet under the sink."

"Thanks."

Carly was glad to have the kitchen to herself. She wasn't sure what had caused her to grab Brand's hand up on the roof. It had felt really nice in her hand. Like hugging him had in the kitchen after he'd said he'd like nothing better than to go beat the shit out of Justin Porter. Words like that could make her insides melt into molten lava if she wasn't careful. He was here to protect her, nothing more. He'd be going away soon enough and she had to remember that. He was a temporary fixture in her life. She reached for her phone and found her favorite playlist, hoping to take her mind off Brand while she cleaned the kitchen.

She was doing well until a soul remake of an eighties tune *Killing me Softly* came on, which made her very aware of the water running in the bathroom and Brand standing under the shower head. The beatbox rhythm made her begin to sway and before she knew it she was dancing and singing along with the soloist, lost in the song and the feel of the tune. She hit replay on her phone and went to her room, not realizing the water had stopped running or that Brand would be in there with only a towel wrapped around his waist, still dripping wet.

"Oh my God. I'm sorry."

Rushing back into the living room, she collapsed on the sofa, trying not to laugh at her reaction and the surprised look on his face when she opened the bedroom door singing at the top of her lungs. There was a reason she didn't make a glee club in high school. It's a wonder he hadn't rushed her, thinking she was crying for help.

# CHAPTER 8

THE NEXT FEW days seemed to go off without a hitch in Carly's mind. She didn't do anything to cause Brand to get upset with her which gave him no reason to be a "hard ass" in Simone's words about everything. He did keep a watch on the surveillance car that came and went. He called Commander Burns on Monday and had a patrol car come around and give the man a ticket. That kept him away for a whole twenty-four hours before he returned. Brand even helped her prepare for her pending interview. She thought that was above and beyond his reason for being there. Yet, she appreciated every minute he spent with her making her feel ready for the appointed time.

But that didn't make her feel less shaky now that the morning had arrived. She drank a little coffee trying to calm her nerves but found it did little to soothe her tummy. All she really wanted was to get in the SUV waiting on them downstairs and get the interview over.

"Okay, Carly, I have the all clear from Hawkeye. The patrol unit has checked out the address where you'll be interviewing. It looks safe for us to arrive at your appointment time. How are you feeling?" Brand asked, coming out of the bathroom wearing his new black suit purchased for the occasion. He'd even picked up a decent looking briefcase at a thrift store to pull off the look.

She found it hard to form her words as she felt her jittery butterflies turn into those of blatant desire. She silently groaned forcing, herself to focus on his questions about how she felt, finally getting her words out. "N-nervous. I haven't been on a job interview since college. That was before I found out Justin Porter didn't want me working outside the home once we married. He conveniently waited until after we said 'I do' and returned from the honeymoon to spring that on me. So, I had to turn down excellent job offers. Stab one at my ego."

"No talking about him today. Clean slate, remember? This is all about you and your new world. Minus what happened at the Pied Piper."

"Right." She slipped on her smart, navy suit jacket that went with the navy pencil skirt she wore with a sleeveless, collarless white blouse that opened in a pleated V-neck. Her navy two-inch heels finished her ensemble with a navy satchel bag containing her resume and business cards, as well as her purse items.

"What if I bomb this?" she said as they walked out the door. She shakily locked it before slipping the key in her bag.

"Don't talk like that. You've got this. We've practiced for the last two days on every possible interview question that could be asked. You did great for me."

"That's because you really weren't the interviewer."

"Carly, you're incorrigible." Brand took her hand and grinned as they went outside.

"I see our private dick is still here."

"Yep. He can't take the hint to get lost."

"Oh well." Carly stepped closer to Brand planning to kiss him on the cheek to give Ragsdale something to really photograph. But Brand turned toward her, and the kiss landed on his lips instead. He pulled her to him and returned the kiss far longer than she ever would have imagined for the private eye's benefit, before breaking away.

She blinked, trying to find her breath for a moment as he opened the SUV door. Instead of sitting up front with the driver, whom she'd learned was Kevin Petree, a rookie detective, Brand followed her into the back and rode to the interview beside her. He didn't say a word about the kiss or why he'd kissed her that way in return, so she decided not to mention it either.

"I will get out at the corner so I can enter the building separate from you. Hopefully, the sidewalk will be crowded enough that no one will notice we both exit the same vehicle."

"Surely they won't." She glanced over and saw he was texting on his phone. "Any news on Colleen or Jules?"

"Not a peep from either Kincaid or McLeod. I have to assume that means things are going well on their end. Donovan has been quiet as well, which is a blessing since we both know your friend Simone comes across as a handful."

Carly giggled, recalling the last thing her friend said to her before they'd parted ways on Saturday. "Donovan may be tied up and not able to contact you if Simone has had her way with him."

"Had her way with him?" Brand said the words still looking at his phone then he looked up. "Shit. You don't think she has a pair of those furry handcuffs do you?"

"She might have more than that, knowing Simone."

Brand groaned, putting his phone down. He turned in the seat, facing her. "Carly, you shouldn't put those wicked thoughts in my head as to what your friend might have done to my guy. He may be in serious danger over there."

"Or he may be deliriously happy."

Brand's brow creased as if he was thinking hard on that for a moment. "Jules isn't like that, is she? I shouldn't worry about McLeod?"

"No. She might get him drunk on single-malt scotch, her favorite drink when she is brooding, but she isn't anything like Simone. And you know that Kincaid is probably still at the hospital with Colleen unless they have released her. You haven't heard anything on that?"

"No." Brand swiveled back around and relaxed beside her for a few miles before he started sending anxious texts.

Carly bit her bottom lip and tried not to laugh. It was endearing how worried he was about his men. She finally reached her hand over and took his, giving it a squeeze. "I'm sure they're fine."

He gave a soft, throaty grunt.

All too soon, the SUV slowed and pulled over to the corner. "This is me. Good luck up there." Brand got out and closed the door.

The driver pulled away from the curb, drove to the front of the building where Carly was going, before stopping again. "Have Brand call when you are ready to be picked up."

"Will do, Kevin. Thanks." She slid toward the door before opening it to get out. She straightened her clothes, took a deep breath, and crossed the pedestrian traffic, then entered the building.

Her heels made clunking sounds on the marble floor as she walked toward the bank of elevators. She waited for Brand to catch up with her before she pressed the up button. Scanning the marque on the wall, she looked for her destination, Stella Stone Interior Designs.

They boarded with several other business-clad men and women and rode in silence to the twelfth floor. Carly didn't look at him. She was afraid she would lose her nerve for the interview or ask him about the kiss back at her apartment building. She quickly pushed that out of her mind, not having time to think about what it meant now. She was almost certain she was going to make it into more than it was anyway. Even if her body sure had felt like it meant more the way she'd come alive, but she didn't have time to think about that. No. Not right now. Focus on the job interview. Focus.

Oh, whom was she kidding? The man was sex in a suit and she'd been living with him for days in her tiny little apartment. Showering where he showered and when she was in there, she was beginning to feel like Simone. Having all sorts of naughty thoughts and imagining what she could do with those furry handcuffs.

Finally, the elevator pinged the twelfth floor. As soon as the doors slid open, Carly was out of there like it was the starting gate opening at the Kentucky Derby. She thought she heard the low rumble of Brand's chuckle behind her, but she didn't care. Her interview awaited. The further she was from him and his intoxicating cologne the better.

BRAND WATCHED Carly go up to the receptionist and give her name while he settled in the waiting area. He took out his cell phone and pretended he was where he needed to be. She was as fidgety as a kitten for some reason and he didn't know why. They'd prepped and he was certain she'd nail this interview. But it was an interview and everyone dealt with stress differently. Like that kiss earlier. He'd only meant to give her a peck on the cheek for good luck, but instead, it had turned out to be a lot more. That in itself could be why she was acting the way she was, though she had kissed him back. So it made sense she'd planned to kiss him as well for a show for Ragsdale? And it backfired on them both.

Boy had it backfired.

He glanced up from his phone and watched as Carly took a seat across the space from him. She sat, crossed her legs and showed off plenty of knee as her skirt rose with the movement. She was busy rearranging her jacket and didn't notice the rise of her skirt. Oh, now she did and she caught him watching. He saw some color flood her cheeks before he looked away.

His phone pinged. It was a message from Hawkeye.

Funeral services for Pied Piper bartender tomorrow. 11 a.m. at Christ's Church on Hollandale if Carly still wants to come. Police will be in full force.

Thanks. Will let her know. At interview now. Over.

A door opened off the side of the open floor plan and a woman came out, "Carly Manning."

He watched as she stood, smoothed out her skirt, and secured the shoulder strap of her satchel. She walked toward the woman exchanging pleasantries with her.

"It's a pleasure to finally meet you, Ms. Manning. I'm Stella Stone." The brown-haired woman shook her hand. "Please follow me to my office."

Carly followed her down a long corridor with framed monochromatic photographs of design projects on the wall. Finally, they came to the woman's office and went inside. It was large, with a glass desk, leather chair, and matching leather guest chairs. Three of the four walls were white; the other was a bank of floor to ceiling windows, which let in ample lighting.

"Please, have a seat. I was very impressed with your interview materials even though you haven't had the job experience of our other applicants since you graduated with your degree. Your application letter explained why, but I'd like to hear more about that if you don't mind. Was it truly your choice when you married?"

Carly took the seat she was offered. "No. I had to pass up several excellent job offers because my husband informed me after the wedding he wanted me dedicated to supporting him and his career. At first, it looked like a fulfilling stepping-stone to raising our family, but that wasn't in the cards. Turns out he didn't want a family. That would have taken me away from devoting all my time to him."

"I see. And is that why the marriage ended?"

"I'm sorry. I'm not sure I see the relevance of why my marriage ended and these interview questions?"

The woman smiled. "Curiosity really. I'm trying to figure out why anyone's ex-husband would go to the lengths he has to make sure you get this job. He has called me not once, but twice this week to ensure that you have a glowing recommendation from him. He wanted to make sure you got this job."

"Justin Porter has been in contact with you?" Carly clutched her satchel tightly in her lap. She swallowed hard, her mouth feeling dry. There was a sickness in the pit of her stomach and she found it difficult to breathe. "I-I don't understand how he even knew I had applied for a job here, let alone that I was interviewing today. I only learned recently he has a P.I. watching my apartment building. Now to discover he knew about this interview is too much. My ex-husband is a very controlling man, Ms. Stone. If he has already contacted you, he will feel he has a right to watch me if I get this job. As much as I'd love to work here for you," Carly paused for a moment, shaking her head and standing up. "I'm sorry. I don't think we can finish this interview."

"Let's not act too hasty, Ms. Manning." Ms. Stone rose as well. "I can assure you, I'd never report back to your ex-husband no matter what he tried. That is not the reason I even brought it up, so you can put that worry to rest. As I see it, there is no reason that you can't work here in the future after you have gained more experience. For now, I'd like you to consider working with another designer I know to get some experience first. Build up your portfolio. I took the liberty of recommending you to her."

"You did?"

Ms. Stone nodded, reaching for a framed photo on her desk. "She's my daughter and in a similar relationship that you have gotten out of, but she won't see reason from her mother. They are not married but engaged. If you can help her see the mistake she is about to make before she does marry him, that will be wonderful."

"But how did you know that is what I'd been through?"

"History repeats itself, Ms. Manning. I was in an abusive relationship at one time and now my daughter is in one. I have never shared that time in my life with her because I never wanted her to know the truth about her father. He died when she was very young. I didn't want it to taint her memory of him. He was ill and the illness caused his abuse, or at least we believed that was the cause back then. I was certain when I read your application that was what I was reading between the lines. When your ex-husband started calling, it confirmed my suspicion for me at least. I wanted to hear it from your lips first."

Ms. Stone set down the picture frame and picked up a business card. "Here is my daughter's card. Brittany will be expecting a phone call from you. I'd be careful where I made the call from."

Carly nodded, stood, and took the card. "Thank you."

Slipping the card in her satchel, Carly hurried from the office, down the corridor, and out into the waiting room. She didn't bother glancing in Brand's direction as she left the office. She was pacing in front of the bank of elevators taking deep, calming breaths when he joined her.

"Carly, what is wrong? What happened in there?"

She looked up at him. "Justin Porter."

"Porter? I don't understand."

"He knew. Somehow, he knew I was interviewing here. He called her. He wanted to give her a glowing recommendation for me." Dropping her satchel, she shook her hands in front of her and huffed in and out. "I'll never be safe living here. I need to leave Chicago. I need to go somewhere far, far away."

Brand stepped into her personal space and pulled her to him. "Sh-h-h, it'll be okay. Porter will not lay a hand on you."

~

CARLY WAS TOO quiet on the ride back to her apartment for Brand's liking. He couldn't tell what she was thinking, but at least he'd gotten her to stop talking about leaving the city for now. She had to testify for Hawkeye in the murder trial first, but once that was over, Brand would take her to Montana if that was where she wanted to go. *If* she wanted to go away with him.

Whoa! What was he even thinking? As soon as this case was over, he was certain the woman would be glad to be as far away from him as she could get. Why would she even want to be around another male after the way Justin Porter had treated her?

Damn. She even had him referring to her ex-husband by his full name.

The SUV slowed to a stop in front of Carly's apartment and he opened the door to get out from behind the driver. He noticed right away that Ragsdale's car sat across the street, but the P.I. wasn't in it. That alarmed him. He leaned back in and spoke to Petree. "Do you mind parking and coming up with us. I might need back up."

"Sure thing, Brand."

"What's going on?" Carly asked, coming alert for the first time since they got in the SUV.

"I'm not sure. Stick close to my side and do what I say without question. Got it?"

She nodded, getting out on her side of the SUV and closing the door.

Brand hurried around the front of the vehicle and

ushered her inside the building. They waited on Petree to join them before proceeding upstairs.

"Take off those heels," Brand ordered.

"What?"

"Do you want to announce to whoever might be upstairs that we're coming? You can hear the clicking of those shoes a mile away on the marble tile flooring in this building."

"Oh." She picked the shoes up and slipped them into her satchel.

When Petree joined them, they took the stairs instead of the elevator so their arrival wouldn't be broadcast. Brand led the way with Carly in the middle and Petree covered her six. There was no way anyone was going to get to her without taking one of them out first.

Ragsdale was picking the lock to her apartment when they reached the landing to her floor.

"Hold it right there," Brand said.

The man halted.

"Step away from the door."

"This isn't what it looks like." Ragsdale held his hands up in surrender. He was wearing latex gloves so he wouldn't leave fingerprints behind. "I was listening to surveillance when I heard something suspicious going on inside. I came up to make sure no harm was going to come to the lady. I'm hired to watch her and not let anything happen to her."

"So Justin Porter had you bug my apartment?" Carly

said. "And you think that makes it all right? You think you can listen into private conversations and it doesn't mean anything? That you aren't violating people by doing it?"

Without warning, Carly ran toward the man so fast Brand had a split second to holster his weapon and catch her around the waist before she leapt onto Ragsdale.

"Let. Me. Go." She twisted in his arms, fighting against him with all her might. Her face was tinged red and her arms were reaching toward Ragsdale as if she wanted to claw his eyes out.

Her bottom wiggled against his groin in a provocative manner and all he wanted to do was drop her, but he didn't dare for fear she would do Ragsdale bodily harm. He'd never seen her so angry.

"Hold it, Carly. Let's hear the man out. If he says he heard something inside your apartment then we should check it out. "

"But why's he picking the lock?" Petree asked.

"Good question." Carly jabbed her elbow into Brand's solar plexus and he grunted, letting her go in reflex. "How'd this imaginary someone get inside if you have to pick the lock?"

Brand watched, ready to move into action again but Carly kept her emotions in control, questioning the P.I. instead of attacking him.

"They were careful and locked the door back when they left," Ragsdale said. "Listen, I was a city detective for many years. I've seen it all before. Break-ins that didn't look like anyone had been there. This is one of them. I'm sure of it."

"Then let's see for ourselves." Carly fished her keys out and unlocked the door. She turned the knob and pushed on the door, which was reluctant to budge. She looked back at Brand and he stepped forward, giving it a shoulder push to open on what looked like a warzone. The living room furniture turned over. Bar stools here and there. She dropped her satchel by the door and before Brand could stop her, she wandered further into the apartment.

The pantry door was open. Cans of food had been tossed onto the floor. Her few dishes were broken into pieces.

Brand saw her bottom lip begin to tremble as she picked up the mismatched plates that were no more and held them close to her chest. She'd taken such pride in those plates.

Ragsdale walked into the kitchen. "Do you hear hissing?"

"What?" Brand turned toward the P.I.

"Hissing. That is what I kept hearing on the surveillance after it got quiet in here. I couldn't tell what was going on but I knew something bad was going down."

"I'm calling this into Commander Burns," Petree said.

"Thanks." Brand crossed over to where Carly stood.

He tried to take the broken dishes from her, but she wouldn't let go of them. A single tear had started streaming down her face, so he backed off, afraid if he tried to comfort her the flood gates would open and she'd break down for sure.

"There it is again," Ragsdale said. "Did you hear it that time?"

Brand pivoted and nodded. "Is it coming from the kitchen?"

The other man stepped carefully around the debris on the floor, going deeper into the tiny workspace. He peered into the sink and then recoiled. "Oh my God."

"What is it?"

"Snakes. Two cobras. The calling card of the Twin Cobra gang."

A whimper escaped from Carly and Brand turned to see her sinking to the floor. How in the hell had that gang found her so fast?

# CHAPTER 9

CARLY SAT in the middle of her stripped bed to make sure there were no hidden surprises in the sheets, trying to wrap her head around what had happened. How had the gang that had shot Phil at the Pied Piper Bar found her? How had they broken into her apartment and left twin cobra snakes in her kitchen sink, turning her apartment into an active crime scene?

Animal Control came to collect the snakes. A crime scene unit dusted for prints and took photographs of the wreckage that had once been her tidy home. Detectives combed through her apartment to make sure there were no more surprises.

Her head had already been spinning after the interview when she learned Justin Porter had called Stella Stone trying to get her the job. Then she came home to find Ragsdale picking her lock because Justin Porter had had him bug her apartment. That had turned out good because Ragsdale had overheard the break-in and knew something dirty had gone down while she was away. But it still didn't make what Justin Porter did right. She would get a restraining order against him. She would find a way to get one if it was the last thing she did. Either that or she'd leave Chicago. That was still an option. After this was all over she could leave Chicago. There was nothing holding her here. Other than Jules, Simone, and Colleen. But they could keep in touch no matter where she lived.

"You still doing okay?" Brand asked, popping into her room.

She slowly nodded.

"Commander Burns is here and he is talking about moving you to a safe house until the trial. Are you okay with that?"

"A safe house?"

"An undisclosed location that no one knows."

"If you think that is what we should do."

"It is. Go ahead and start packing your clothes. Be sure to pack something for the funeral."

"The funeral?" Her pulse began to race.

"Phil's funeral. You still want to go, don't you?"

"Oh. Yes. I do. I'd forgotten. I – I guess when you said funeral I thought you meant mine."

He grinned. "That's not going to happen. So don't even think that."

"After today, I wouldn't be so sure."

"Things may look grim, but they will get brighter,"

he said, coming over to where she sat. "May I sit with you?"

She nodded and scooted for him to join her.

He took her hand in his. "I was shot in theater which left a piece of shrapnel lodged too close to a blood vessel in my chest that can't be removed. I'm physically fine, but it's too risky for active duty. I thought my world had ended when I got the news that I couldn't be a SEAL anymore. I went into a black hole in my mind. I thought my life was over. There was nothing left for me. Then one day as I was recuperating at Walter Reed I got this phone call from Hank Patterson. I didn't know the man. Never heard of him before. Yet that one little phone call from him changed my life, Carly. He offered me a job with the Brotherhood Protectors doing what I couldn't do for the SEALs. I'm working with former SEALs or Army Rangers or Marines that have been wounded or retired out that still want to serve their country with their skills. The Brotherhood Protectors allows us to do that. So what looks bleak right now can change tomorrow. Give it time. It will get better."

She swallowed, squeezing his hand. "When is Phil's funeral again?"

"Tomorrow."

"Do you think it will be safe for me to go?"

"There will be plenty of Chicago PD and detectives there. You'll be safe. And you've got me. I'm not going to let anyone get to you while I'm still breathing."

"Okay." She tried to smile.

By late afternoon, everyone had departed from Carly's apartment. Ragsdale had even left, giving his word not to follow them when they moved to the undisclosed location. Brand wasn't sure if he believed the P.I., though he'd take his word for it and keep an eye out as well to make sure they weren't tailed.

Brand helped Carly take her luggage to the lobby and get it into the SUV. Then he loaded his own duffle and tactical bag that hadn't been touched when the Twin Cobras had trashed the apartment. They'd thankfully stayed to the living room and kitchen area. Petree brought out the two laundry baskets full of food items from the refrigerator and freezer they were taking with them, as well as canned items from the pantry since they didn't know how long they'd be gone.

They traveled in silence across town to the safe house as the sun began to set, giving off a rosy orange glow over the harbor. Petree drove around for longer than necessary it seemed to Brand before he finally turned down Lakeshore Drive and pulled to a stop in front of an apartment building.

"Are you sure we're at the right location?" Carly asked.

"This is the address Commander Burns texted me.

A Margot Wills should be waiting for you inside with the keys."

"Margot Wills as in Senator Wills daughter?"

Petree turned around from the front seat to look at her. "I guess so. I didn't put two and two together, but now that you mention it."

"Is there a problem, Carly?" Brand asked.

"No. We were sorority sisters in college. I can trust her to keep my whereabouts secret."

"Then let's go meet her." Brand opened the door and got out, waiting for Carly to slide out of the SUV.

A deep chestnut haired woman in a one-piece sunburst-bathing suit with a matching sarong wrapped around her waist and strappy heels greeted them. "Carly Manning! Darling, it has been too long. I had no idea I'd be meeting you here today. When Burnsie called daddy needing a favor, we were only too happy to help out. We aren't using the furnished apartment right now. Daddy only keeps it around for when he and Mumsie dearest number five are on the outs and he needs a place to get away."

"Burnsie?" Brand said.

Margot batted her fake eyelashes at him. "Yes, do you know him?"

"I do."

"Put in a good word for me then."

"He's married."

"That is irrelevant. One day he may not be and he'd remember your good word."

"The apartment?" Carly asked.

"Yes. Come this way. It's on the top floor. Excellent view of the skyline. The balcony opens up to a gorgeous patio area for entertaining. Sometimes I think that is why my father bought the place. Daddy had the whole place renovated last year and put in a new marble shower with all new fixtures in the bathroom. If I didn't have my own apartment in this building I'd be clamoring for his."

"So you live here as well."

Margot nodded. "I've been sunbathing by the pool. I don't go around town like this, though I do have the body for it."

"You haven't changed, Margot. Still a spit-fire."

The woman giggled as the elevator doors slid open and the three of them stepped inside. She slid a key into the panel on the right and pressed the 20th-floor button. "You'll have to do that to access your floor. Otherwise, no one can get up there. It's another security measure my father had installed, being a senator and all. You can't be too careful." She turned to Carly without taking a breath. "I heard you and Porter divorced. Such a tragedy when young love goes sour."

"Doesn't it make entertaining difficult?" Carly asked, ignoring her last statement.

"No. Daddy has a service run the elevator all night, screening guests and only letting those on the list up. Works perfectly. The other tenants hate it though."

"What about the stairs? Couldn't someone get up there easy enough?" Brand asked.

"Not without a key. You can go up and down to the 19th floor all you want, but you have to have two keys to get into the 20th stairwell door. They are on this key ring too. I'll show you from the hallway that leads to the stairs outside the apartment."

Margot did that and more when they arrived on the 20th floor. Brand busied himself checking on the security aspect of the apartment while Carly and Margot scoped out the amenities. He didn't care how luxurious the place was for their comfort as long as he had a place to sleep, water to shower and could prepare food to eat. So what if the place had a state of the art kitchen, open floor plan and floor to ceiling windows all along the perimeter wall giving an ample skyline view. Which in Margot's words meant location, location, location real-estate wise. He noticed that the windows were triple-thick, shatterproof glass for security measures. The senator was no fool. Brand was more concerned where this door off from the kitchen led.

He turned the knob but the door wouldn't budge. "Where does this door go to?"

"That leads up to the sky roof where there is a helipad. Another one of daddy's necessities as a senator. Gotta get to the state capital right away he can whisk away in his helicopter. Need to get to DC but if traffic is horrible to O'Hare he takes his helicopter. Men and their toys."

Brand grunted. Men and their toys indeed. That might come in handy if they needed a speedy getaway. "I assume we'll have a key to this door as well, in case of an emergency helicopter exit?"

"Of course." Margot held up the key ring full of keys and shook it at him. "They're all labeled. This is my set. Daddy has the other. You'll be perfectly safe here. Burnsie wouldn't have asked for you to stay if you weren't."

"Thank you, Margot." Carly touched her arm. "We do appreciate it."

"I don't know what kind of trouble you are in, Carly, but you have my sympathy. I don't think I could sleep at night."

"Be glad you don't have my worries right now."

KEVIN AND BRAND brought up the luggage and food while Carly was ordered to stay in the apartment for her own safety. After the day she'd had, she didn't really have much of a fight left in her to protest. She curled up on the leather sofa and laid her head against it, watching the sun sink into the fading light. Sometime later, she opened her eyes, surprised she had drifted off to sleep, only waking to the clatter of pots and pans Brand and Kevin made in the kitchen.

"What's going on over there?" she asked, slowly uncurling her legs.

"We're making comfort food," Kevin said. "My momma's homemade vegetable soup and primo deli grilled cheese sandwiches."

"Primo?" She sniffed the air, savoring the delicious aroma that filled the apartment.

"Yeah, there's this gourmet deli down the street that makes grilled cheese sandwiches with Gouda and Asiago cheese on artisan bread. I was on a case with another detective and we ate there once. I ran down and purchased the ingredients to make our own. If we're on Lakeshore, we might as well eat like we are on Lakeshore, right?"

Carly laughed. She believed this was the most she'd heard Kevin Petree talk the whole time he'd been driving her and Brand around this week. "Might as well."

"You have a good nap?" Brand finally asked. He hadn't taken his eyes off her since she'd joined them in the kitchen area.

Nodding, she glanced at him, feeling heat flood through her from his gaze. "It helped me feel less tense about today. Maybe I'll rest better tonight."

"Momma's soup should do the trick," Kevin said going back to the gas range to flip the sandwiches. He turned the flame down to low, then ladled three bowls of soup for them.

"I'll go freshen up," Carly said, heading down the

hall to the master bedroom. She found her suitcase lying on the bed and her makeup case sitting beside it. Taking the smaller bag into the bathroom, she opened it up and took out her brush, making sure her hair wasn't too messy from the nap on the couch. She freshened her makeup too before heading back to the kitchen.

A glass of tea and a bowl of soup waited for her beside Brand at the counter. Kevin was slicing the grilled cheese sandwiches diagonally with a large knife and placed them on the counter as well before taking his place on the opposite side of Carly.

She felt like a protection detail sandwiched between the two men. All safe and sound. She wondered if Kevin was going to start sleeping here now that there was more space than her tiny apartment, but she didn't voice her question. It wasn't up to her. That was a Brand call. If Brand thought they needed the extra man for security purposes, then she was certain Kevin would be here.

The three of them ate in comfortable silence for most of the meal. Until Brand and Kevin began discussing the latest baseball stats. They even talked about catching a game together at Wrigley Field once the case was over. Carly felt like an invisible spot they were talking over. She finished her food so she could get out of their way.

She cleaned up in the kitchen while they talked, refilled their bowls, and poured more tea without them even noticing. It made her feel like she was back to her old routine at Justin Porters and that made her cringe. No. No. No. This is nothing like that. Brand and Kevin were finally getting to know one another after a week of the man serving as only their driver. Today he'd played a vital role in saving her life with Brand and they were bonding. That was all.

Why did it bother her that she was no longer Brand's focus? *Because it had felt nice to have had his total attention.* She'd lost that with Justin Porter too soon after they married. She realized that now.

She finished up in the kitchen and slipped down the hallway to the bedroom again. The closet was empty. She began hanging up clothes and putting things away on the shelves since there was no chest in the room for her foldable items. It was all part of the modern look of the apartment.

Brand knocked on her door twenty minutes later. "Can I come in?"

"Sure."

"Kevin's gone for the night. We didn't expect you to clean up. We didn't even realize you were doing it as we talked."

She shrugged. "No problem."

"Are you upset about something?"

"It's been a long, upsetting day all around. I'm not upset about one thing, Brand, I'm upset about lots of things. None of them about you or Kevin ignoring me at dinner, talking about baseball, forgetting I was even in the room. If I were, that would be pretty shallow, now wouldn't it?"

He cocked his head to the side and creased his brow. "So you're saying you're not upset about that, but everything else that happened today?"

"Yes."

"Just making sure. Because we really didn't mean to exclude you in the conversation."

"Not everything has to be about me."

"See, when you make comments like that I get the feeling you are pissed at me."

"Well...maybe I'm pissed at the male population in general, which unfortunately you happen to be one of. My world has been shattered for the second time this year, okay. No...third time if you take into account what happened at the bar. I have nowhere that I truly feel safe because of Justin Porter and the Twin Cobra gang. Nowhere."

"Yes, you do."

Brand closed the distance between them and pulled her tight against his chest, wrapped her safely in his strong arms. "Right here. That is where you are safe. I will not let anyone do you harm."

Her breath caught in her throat for a moment as she relished the security she felt, but she was a smart woman. This was a temporary situation here. "That is good for now, Brand, but you won't always be here. I'm an assignment. That is all. I know that. Once I testify your job will be done."

She felt him tense at her words.

HOW COULD she think she was only a job to him? Hadn't he told her he would protect her with his life? Sure, that was his job, but he'd meant it as far more when he'd said it, didn't she realize it? It was clear she hadn't taken it that way. What more did she want from him?

He released her, stepping away. "I'll go unpack."

"Oh…okay." She stepped back as well, crossing her arms and hugging herself.

She looked confused. The same way he felt, but he didn't know what to say to her at the moment, so he left the room. He needed to think and he couldn't do it with her so close. He was glad his room was on the opposite side of the kitchen to put distance between them.

Traveling down the hallway, he tried to understand why he was feeling this way about her. He'd never let an assignment get this close to him before that he became so emotionally messed up inside. Too bad he hadn't thought to find out from Margot if there was a workout room in the complex. He could bench-press some weights or go a few rounds with the punching bag. Maybe then, he could figure out why he was having these feelings for Carly.

Maybe he could even figure out why the feelings

were happening. Had he changed? Or was it the situation? Or had this woman somehow wormed her way into his soul where no one else had ever been able to go?

The only possible way Carly had been able to worm her way in was if he'd let his guard down. He was a Navy SEAL. He didn't let his guard down.

Questions about this possibility swam in his head as he opened up the closet and hung up a few clothes beside the garment bag containing the suit he'd purchased just so he'd be able to play his role while she went on her interview. A clear sign he was going soft. Whenever would he have purchased a new suit for undercover work? He'd spent hours shopping to make sure he'd gotten a good deal and the right fit. In the end, he'd chosen a black so it would serve him a long time. As well as a couple of shirts and ties to go with it and new dress shoes.

He unzipped his duffle and shoved his foldable clothes on the open shelves as fast as he could not wanting to think it was possible that he had let his guard down. The only way he'd ever have done that is if he had feelings for Carly. But how? When? Had it happened gradually as he'd gotten to know her this week?

He saw a flash of her cracking that whip when he walked into her apartment on Saturday morning. Then her showing him the garden spot on the rooftop of her building. The hours they'd spent preparing for her interview. The accidental kiss this morning before her interview, then that long, agonizing drive having to pretend it didn't happen. Had it only been this morning? It seemed so much longer than eight hours ago.

There was a tightness in his chest that formed in a flash of a second as he recalled her clutching the pieces of her tag sale dishes, refusing to let go. He swallowed the taste of raw emotion bubbling up in his throat. And he was tempted to run back across the apartment to her. Damn it to hell. This wasn't happening to him. How could he be objective and protect her without letting his emotions get in the way?

He was a former SEAL for Christ sakes. He wasn't supposed to let emotions get in the way. He was all about the job, nothing but the job. Carly was the job.

But, he couldn't live with himself if something happened to her. Hell, he already knew he didn't want to live without her in his life. Job or no job.

Storming out of his room, he headed back to her, calling her name as he picked up speed, closing the distance between them. "Carly. Carly."

"Brand?" She met him with a questioning look at her doorway. Her cheeks were glistening wet as if she'd been crying.

*Had his leaving made her cry?"* Dammit.

He didn't let that stop him. He was a man on a mission. Cupping her face with palms up under her chin, he lowered his lips to hers, tasting the salty tears on her lips as he kissed her harder than he intended.

She hungrily responded, opening for him to slip his tongue into her mouth and taste her fully.

Her warm body pressed instantly against his and he could feel the swell of her breasts. She ran her hands up his hard six-pack, to his chest, and then around his neck, pulling him closer as their tongues tangled in their warm haven.

Letting his hands roam down her back to her bottom, he lifted her and she wrapped her legs around his waist as he carried her further into the room, over to her bed where he turned slightly and sat down, never breaking their contact.

She pulled away catching her breath and smiled at him.

"You're more than a job to me, Carly. You stopped being a job…that's all I know. I don't want you to think you're just a job to me."

"I shouldn't have said that, Brand. I was upset. I am upset thinking about how things will be different once the job is over. The thought of losing you upsets me."

"Who says you have to lose me?"

"Don't tease me."

"I'm not."

# CHAPTER 10

CARLY WOKE the next morning curled up beside Brand, lying on the bed with a thin afghan thrown over them. She scooted closer to him and he wrapped a protective arm around her. Closing her eyes, she recalled their kiss the night before that made her feel as if he'd bared his soul to her. The way he'd held her in his arms and carried her over to the bed before he'd sat down with her. He could have laid her on the bed, but he hadn't. He didn't try to dominate her. He let her guide where and how far they had gone. When she'd asked him to stay and sleep in her room after the scare of the day he'd wanted to sleep in the armchair. But, she'd insisted that they sleep on top of the comforter because she'd needed him near.

The buzzing of his phone woke Brand and he pulled away from her, rolling off the bed. He grabbed his shoes as he answered the call.

"Good morning, Hawkeye." Brand looked back at her and winked. "Sure, we can be ready in an hour for the motor detail to pick us up. Absolutely. We'll see you then."

"Did we sleep that late?" She scrambled off the bed on the other side and began looking for her own cellphone.

"It's already ten. The service is at noon."

"I haven't slept this late since I had the flu."

"I'm positive I was in high school," he said, jamming his phone in his pocket.

Carly laughed trying to imagine him as a teen. Was he a jock or one of those ivy-league wannabe preppy types? He had to be smart to be a Devgru SEAL, right? Her curiosity died with her laughter. She couldn't bring herself to ask. It didn't matter what he was back then. All that mattered was what he was now. And that he made her feel safe and alive for the first time in a long time.

It struck her then that she knew very little about him. Yet, she already knew she never wanted to spend another day without him in her life. Was that a rational thing to desire? Or had her experience with Justin Porter drove her to live in the moment?

"I better go shower. You had too."

His words jarred her out of thought. She realized she'd been standing there staring at him this whole time as her mind drifted. "Right. Yeah. Of course."

"Carly, are you okay?" He cocked his head to the side, not taking his eyes off her.

Her face heated and she was certain it had flushed with color as well. "Thinking about...oh...never mind." She pointed toward the doorway that led to her bathroom. "I'm going to go shower now."

He grinned, taking a quick step to her and planting a kiss on her forehead. "You are adorable when you get flustered."

She raised her right hand up to her brow and gave a quick salute. Then she dashed to her bathroom to the sound of his chuckle.

CARLY OPTED NOT to take a purse with her to the funeral. She applied her extended wear lipstick before they left the apartment on Lakeshore and got into the police detail caravan. Despite the many days since the shooting, Carly couldn't help but relive it all once again on the extremely quiet drive over sitting beside Brand and holding his hand. She couldn't even pretend they were only going to church because as soon as they approached Christ's Church on Hollandale there were police SUVs, cars and even swat vehicles parked in the parking lot, up and down the main and side streets where Phil's funeral was being held. Local television station vans were parked across the street and one was even lucky enough to get into the business next-door's parking lot to provide live coverage of the event for the noon and evening news.

Their driver was someone other than Kevin Petree today. He drove up to the front of the church and dropped them off with the other two men in black who rode with them. Kevin met them at the church and walked inside with them. He was wearing an earwig, a black suit and he had on dark sunglasses like the other men. Once again, Carly was a security sandwich between Brand and Kevin, but she didn't mind it out in the open where she was a target.

She looked around the church then leaned closer to Brand. "I don't see Simone. Isn't she coming?"

"Negative. She didn't want to."

"Oh. I just assumed."

"Not everyone is as caring as you," Brand said.

Carly tried to smile at what he said as they stood in line to pay their respects. The line was much longer than she imagined, but it made her feel proud to know that Phil had this many people who turned out for him in the end. She'd only met him that one night. She was certain there were many patrons of the Pied Piper that came on a regular basis who had to be there, sitting in the pews.

Finally, they made it to the front, where the casket draped with a floral spray sat and his widow stood. She didn't look much older than Carly. She had dark hair and warm brown eyes and had the same olive complexion as Phil. Commander Burns came forward from the side and said something to the woman before Carly could even speak to her.

She began to cry, nodding her head.

"What's going on?" Carly asked Brand.

"I don't know." He leaned back behind Carly and spoke to Kevin Petree. Carly could hear their muffled whispers, but that was all she could make out over the sound of the voices in the church and the soft piano music.

A woman on her left side handed his widow a box of tissues and she pulled several out. She wiped her eyes and blew her nose as the commander spoke to her. At last, he looked up at Carly and motioned for her to step forward.

"Carly, this is Phil's widow, Carmen," Commander Burns said. "She's wanted to meet you since Friday night."

"I wanted to thank you for what you did, but I was told I would have to wait. I can't thank you enough for trying to protect my Phil from that shooter. The Commander told me how you took Phil's bat to him when he wanted to hurt him more."

*Hurt him more? That's not what went down.* Carly decided not to quibble.

"I've wanted to meet you too. I wanted to tell you how special a person I thought your husband was. I only met him that night, but he kept me from drinking too much and another patron of the bar from taking advantage of me when I'd clearly had more than enough to drink. He was a very decent man and you should be proud to call him your husband. I just wish … I just wish things could have turned out differently. He didn't have to die. If I had realized that the shooter had a bullet in the gun after he already pulled the trigger on my friend and nothing fired, maybe I could have acted faster, maybe if I hadn't had so much to drink earlier I would have been thinking more clearly and would have …"

"Gotten yourself killed," Carmen said. She shook her head. "No, Carly. You fighting off the shooter with the bat after he already killed my Phil was all you could do. It's just a shame that your testimony will not be needed now to put him away."

"Wh-hat?" Carly squeaked.

"What's happened? Why won't Carly be testifying against the man that shot Phil?"

"I was just explaining that someone got to the man at the jail and gave him a lethal injection in his cell. He was found with a hypodermic needle still sticking out of his jugular about an hour ago."

"Do you think the Twin Cobras would do this to their own?" Carly asked finding it hard to breathe. She held onto Brand's arm a little tighter and took several small, but deep breaths to try to stay calm.

"We're not sure. We had him in what we considered a secure area away from the general population. If it wasn't them it was one of their rival gangs." Commander Burns looked at both Carly and Carmen.

"Until we find out who was responsible then security will be heightened on both of you."

Carmen wiped her eyes with her tissue and then gave Carly a hug. "Thank you again."

"Bless you. Maybe after all this is over we can get together?"

"Maybe."

Carly and Brand moved on to view the body for a moment. In her mind her few interactions with Phil flashed by stopping on the sound of the gunfire and the spark of the bullet slamming him back against the glass mirror. She closed her eyes, blocking out the images the best she could before Brand ushered her to the pew that was reserved for them with the other law enforcement officials.

"Brand, will I make it out of this alive?" she asked.

"You know the answer to that question."

Carly tried to put everything out of her mind the best she could as she waited for the service to begin., But, when the speaker began to talk about Phil her mind drifted to what would one say about her if this were her service instead? What if she were the one lying in the casket. Would her parents even darken the doors of the church then? Would they even care? Not once since her name had been in the newspaper about the shooting at the Pied Piper had she heard from either of them.

She began to cry, not a few tears that normally happen when you attend someone's funeral, but mega tears. Her nose was running and the floodgates had opened. This was the worst time for this to happen. She was here for Phil. Instead she was becoming a soppy mess as she had a private pity party. She'd held it together as long as she could about her parents. Their resentment toward her about the divorce from Justin. Whether she'd wanted to admit it or not, they're not reaching out to her s was more than she could take. Brand handed her the pack of tissues they'd found at the apartment and she pulled out several, trying to stop the waterworks. She finally pulled it together, grateful she'd worn waterproof mascara or she'd have black streaks down her face.

For the closing prayer, the speaker had everyone stand before dismissing them to follow the procession to the graveside. Carly had no idea if they were going to that or not. She doubted it. That would be too much in the open exposure and all protection needed to be on Carmen and not divided between the two. Besides, she'd done what she'd come here to do. She'd spoken to his widow. She'd gotten to tell her what an impression Phil had made on her, but what she hadn't expected was to find that Carmen wanted to meet her as well. What she didn't understand is why Burns told Carmen that Carly had taken the shooter out with the bat to keep him from shooting Phil again? That wasn't the reason at all. The shooter had been going to shoot Carly for not putting the bat down and getting away from the body. Had Burns misspoken before he'd known the facts and he didn't see the reason to correct himself since it didn't change anything in the end? Or had Carmen misunderstood? Either way, Phil was still dead. Thanks to Carly, they had captured the shooter.

Brand offered his arm to Carly as they walked out of the church. Because of the number of people exiting the building their driver couldn't come and pick them up in the front. Instead, they walked over to the side where the detail sat when shots rang out.

Screams and bullet fire created chaos all around Christ's Church. Brand had Carly down on the pavement so fast it scraped her knees and tore her stockings in the process. People were running for their vehicles. Police officers shouted for people to go back inside the church until the area was secured.

Carly tried to look up, but she couldn't see much other than Brand covering her body with his own. She had no idea if he'd been shot or not. He wasn't moving and that frightened her to no end. Though she found his weight on her didn't bother her.

"Lay still."

His order comforted her more than she thought.

"I thought you were shot."

"No. Now be quiet. I need to listen to what is going on around us."

She did as she was told, even slowing her breathing down. She heard footsteps near them and she thought it sounded like Kevin's light step scraping on the pavement. She turned her head and saw those wingtips he usually wears. He stooped down and looked at her.

"Are the two of you going to lie there all day?"

"Waiting for the all clear," Brand said.

"All clear," Kevin said, offering him a hand up.

They both lifted Carly to her feet.

"Ouch, those knees don't look good. Brand, next time you want to play linebacker with our girl, do it in the grass," Kevin said, trying to make light of the situation.

"You get the shooter?"

"No. He was long gone by the time SWAT found his shooting spot. No casualties though. Lots of scared people. Commander said for you to get Carly to the safe house and stay put until he says otherwise. I'll be driving you back since the bigger guns are going to the graveside."

The parking lot was still chaotic as they walked to the SUV assigned to Kevin. An officer was standing guard of the vehicle. "Thanks, man. I know you'd rather be doing more important jobs than watching my ride all morning, but I appreciate it."

"Keeping you and other officers safe is all part of the job too," the officer said. "If we can't serve each other as well as the public then we don't need to be wearing this uniform."

"You're so right," Kevin said. He opened up the back door for Carly and Brand to get inside before he got into the driver's side.

He backed out of the parking space and drove across the lot toward a side street that fed into Hollandale. The SUV jerked and he swerved. There was a loud boom that reverberated through the vehicle, then whooshing of air. Not once. Not twice. But four times.

Carly screamed. She removed her seat belt and got into the floorboard. Brand followed, shielding her again from any harm. Each time another boom/whoosh sounded, she screamed again.

Kevin slammed the SUV into park and got out cursing a blue streak. He didn't have anything good to say about the officer who had been watching the vehicle.

"Stay here," Brand ordered. He crawled over her and got out to see what was going on. All four tires had blown as they drove.

Officers and detectives came running toward them. Hawkeye included.

"Is Carly okay?" He asked.

"Yeah, she's inside." Brand pointed to the SUV.

"I don't get it. My detail had an officer on guard." Kevin paced, and then kicked the flat tire on the driver's side. He clasped his hands behind his head, looking up to the sky. He turned slowly. "Do you hear that?"

"Hear what?" Brand pushed through the throng of men.

"It sounds like faint ticking."

Brand stepped closer to the vehicle until he could

hear what Kevin was referring. He grabbed the handle on the back passenger door and opened the SUV, pulling Carly out. He ran with her as far away from the parked vehicle as he could while the other men scattered as well and ordered others in the parking lot to do the same.

Within ten seconds, the SUV exploded and what was left of the frame began to burn.

Carly stared in silence, made a sound like a mewling kitten, and then went limp in his arms.

WHEN CARLY CAME AROUND, she was lying on the bed with the afghan over her in the apartment on Lakeshore. It was four in the afternoon and she didn't know how they'd finally made it home from the church. Brand had changed out of his suit and was wearing tactical pants and a black t-shirt, sitting in the armchair in her room. He looked much the way he had the first night she met him, except much softer around the edges.

"Are you hungry?" he asked.

She nodded.

"Good. Kevin made his momma's vegetable soup again and went to the deli down the street and purchased some hero sandwiches for us."

"Is he here?"

"No. He's being reassigned. He had to report to

headquarters for briefings about today. So, the soup and sandwiches are his parting gift to us. Hawkeye thinks he's been targeted as our driver and could lead the Twin Cobras to your door now."

Carly pushed herself up to a sitting position. "If Kevin can be reassigned then what about you?"

"No way. Kevin's our driver. I'm your protector."

"Burns is clear on that? He won't get confused and decide I need Donnie or Wyatt."

"Donnie?" He grinned, shaking his head. "No. He won't get confused. Don't worry. Besides, I'd take you away from Chicago before I'd let him do that."

"You would, would you?"

"Yes, I would."

"Don't I get a say in it?" She got to her knees and wiggled her finger at him to come closer.

He grinned again, closing the distance between them. "I think I can persuade you easy enough."

"Then persuade away." She snaked her arms up around his neck and pulled him down to her. "Persuade away."

# CHAPTER 11

BRAND SUCKED IN HIS BREATH. Carly had no idea what she was doing, telling him to persuade her. She was literally giving him free rein to do what he wished with her, but he wouldn't go that far, not this soon. In his opinion, she was too fragile after everything that had happened to jump into anything too intense. He seriously didn't know how she was holding it together after the emotional rollercoaster she'd been on in the last twenty-four hours. He'd seen SEALs in training not be able to handle similar emotional brutality and flunk out.

For that reason alone, he kissed this amazing woman before him briefly and pulled away.

"Don't stop." She reached for him to instigate another kiss, but he backed away, grabbing her hands and holding them with his own.

"You need to eat first, change out of your ruined

hose and put on something comfortable. Maybe even take another hot shower and relax for the rest of the evening."

She puckered her lips into a little pout. "Is that your best shot at persuasion, Mr. Chambers?"

"No. I haven't even begun because I'm worried about you, Carly. I think you want to instigate sex as a way to forget what has been happening in the last two days. I don't want that to be how things progress between us."

"Really? That's what you think?" She jerked her hands away from him and got off the bed. "Because when you came in here last night and you kissed me I thought you were saying you wanted to take our relationship to the next level. That you cared about me. And if our kissing led to anything more than just kissing would that be so bad?"

"Under normal circumstances, no."

"We didn't meet under normal circumstances, Brand."

"But wouldn't it be better if we let our relationship progress slower and then lead up to the physical naturally instead of you wanting to prove you're still alive after what has happened in the last twenty-four hours?"

She wrinkled her brow, looking confused. "Prove I'm alive?"

"It's like when there is a death. People handle grief

in many ways. Some cope others turn to other vices. Sex is one of them."

Stepping toward him, she touched his cheek with the palm of her hand and he leaned into it. "Have you done that?"

He nodded. "My brother. I was young and stupid. It made me feel whole. Dean was older, smarter, and my hero. But his death, in the end, led me to the SEALs."

"Thank you for sharing that with me, Brand." She leaned down and kissed him on the forehead, then ran her nose along his before capturing his mouth with her own. She straddled him, pressing her heat against his groin.

She wanted him. He knew that. Just as much as he wanted her even if he was trying to slow things down between them to make sure it was for all the right reasons. He knew Carly was special and he didn't want to screw things up with her. Yet something in his brain triggered an impulse move and before he knew it, he had her pinned on the bed with his body.

Instead of her removing her ruined hose, he was the one shimming them down her slender legs, feeling her silky, smooth skin under his rough hands as he ran them up and down the expanse. He was careful around her scraped knees because she flinched when he touched the flesh there. He left her mouth and moved down to the afflicted area, gently administering kiss.

"Sorry for these."

"Hazards of being a witness for the prosecution,"

she replied, her tummy making rumbling noises as he returned to resume their kissing.

He shifted his weight off her and leaned up on his elbows. "You're hungry."

She nodded. "I guess we should go eat Kevin's soup since he was kind enough to make it for us."

"I'll go ladle the bowls and cut the sandwiches while you change out of your dress."

"Sounds like a plan, but I call dibs on returning here for dessert."

He grinned, lifting a hand to his mouth and kissing a spot in the center of her palm. "Your wish is my command."

She giggled and sat up. "Are you my genie?"

"You'll have to wait and see."

BRAND WAS HALFWAY down the hallway to the kitchen when his phone rang. He recognized the number immediately. "Hey, Hawkeye, what's up?"

"I've got some bad news."

"What?" Brand couldn't take any more bad right now. "Just spit it out."

"Headquarters wants to meet about my proposal tonight. They've called a 6 p.m. meeting to discuss it. The team leader did not sound favorable in support of it after what went down at the funeral today. I really need you there to give a demonstration of what your team can do. I've called Margot Wills and she's willing to visit with Carly while you are away."

"Do you think she's the best choice? That woman is a bombshell."

Hawkeye chuckled. "Margot is a handful, but so is Carly's friend Simone. They should get along just fine."

"Oh, I'm sure they will. They were sorority sisters in college."

"I had no idea. So why are you worried?"

"I find Margot a poor choice for protection."

"She's not protection. I'll have plainclothes officers stationed downstairs for that. Besides, Margot tells me no one can get up to the 20th floor without the key, and you have the key."

"True."

"I'll send a car around for you at five so be ready. Oh, and wear your tactical gear to impress the powers that be."

"No problem." Brand ended the call, laid his phone on the counter. He opened up the cabinet, taking down two bowls.

"Was that you on the phone? I thought I heard you talking." Carly came in wearing a pair of faded blue-jean shorts and a t-shirt with lace around the bottom. She'd pulled her hair back in a low ponytail.

"It was Hawkeye. I'm afraid our dessert will have to be postponed until later tonight. I have to go talk to a group of people about the task force he is trying to get approved."

"Then you have to bring chocolate chip salted caramel ice cream back, a can of whip cream and long stem maraschino cherries."

"Anything else?"

"Waffle cone bowls?"

"I'll try to remember all that tall order and not get laughed out of the car when I explain to Hawkeye what I have to stop and get."

She winked at him.

They ate in silence and she cleaned up while he got his gear together. "Oh, I forgot to tell you that Margot is coming up to stay with you so you won't be alone while I'm gone. Hawkeye arranged it."

"I would have been fine by myself, but tell him thank you. It will be nice to get caught up. Yesterday was the first time I'd seen her since my wedding. I didn't even know she was still living in Chicago, but then if she wasn't on Justin Porter's list of approved people I didn't see her. It's surprising that he even allowed me to see Jules, Simone, and Colleen."

Brand stopped in front of her, tilted her chin up with the crook of his bent finger and kissed her. "Rule from now on, let's not say the JP in the apartment unless necessary. Deal?"

"Deal."

As if on cue, a buzzer sounded and then the voice of Margot followed. "Hello. I would like entrance to the 20th floor, please. It's Margot Wills."

"Coming down now. Will meet you on the 19th floor. Come on up."

Brand turned back around and pulled Carly to him one more time, brushing his lips against hers. "I'll be back as soon as I can."

"I know you will. Do well for the task force."

Brand left the apartment, taking the stairs down to the 19th floor and met the elevator with Margot on it. He got on and rode back up to the 20th with her, waited until she was inside with Carly and the lock clicked on the door before he pressed L for the lobby.

"Do you want something to eat?" Carly asked Margot as they came into the apartment.

"I already ate. I was thinking more like a good glass of wine and sitting out on the roof, watching the sun go down." Margot dangled a set of keys for Carly to see. "I brought along my set to daddy's wine cellar.

"Wine cellar? You didn't mention anything about that yesterday."

"Your guy didn't look the wine type."

"Brand."

Margot nodded, going over to the long wall expanse between the kitchen area and the hall leading to the bedroom where Brand was sleeping. She touched the wall on the side and a panel opened exposing a glass door. She unlocked it and went inside.

Curious, Carly followed, amazed at the wooden shelving and the bottles of wine stored in the space at a controlled temperature.

"Another one of your father's renovations to the apartment?"

"Yes. This was a third bedroom that was never in use so he turned it into a wine room. The upgrades will earn a hefty profit when he decides to sell."

"I'd love to live here on a permanent basis."

Margot arched a brow, selecting a bottle of wine from one of the wooden racks. "If it's the building you like as much as the apartment, I know there's space opening up on the eighth floor. Two bedrooms, two baths, open floor plan kitchen, living space without the patio balcony."

"I do. It wouldn't have to be as fancy as this, but I'm going to be starting a new job and could swing the rent. After what happened at my apartment, I know I can't go back there other than to pack my things and leave."

"Then I'll make a call and show you the place tomorrow. I know the tenants and they will be more than happy to let you see their apartment."

Carly smiled. A tightness formed in the pit of her stomach at the thought of moving and taking on higher rent. She still hadn't given Brittany Daniels a call yet about the interior design job. What if she didn't get the job? She needed to do that first thing in the morning before she even looked at the apartment.

"This is our wine for the night," Margot said, showing off a bottle she pulled from the rack. "Daddy has several bottles and he won't miss one of these."

Carly followed her out of the room and then went into the kitchen to get the wine glasses down. Margot locked the door and closed the wall panel back. Carly opened the refrigerator and pulled out the deli Gouda and Asiago cheeses. She washed two apples, sliced those, and laid them on a plate with the cheese. Then she looked in the cabinet for a box of crackers to add a few to the plate.

Margot uncorked the wine, smelled of the cork, and grinned. "I'll let it breathe a few minutes before pouring. Smell of this."

She waved the cork under Carly's nose. "Doesn't that remind you of the wine tasting tour we took at that vineyard in southern France?"

"It does."

"That was the year before you started dating Justin Porter. We had fun before then."

Carly sighed, picking up the plate and wine glasses to carry outside. "It seems like a different life to me."

"Oh, honey. That man did a number on you."

She nodded. "But I don't speak of him here. I promised Brand."

"Speaking of men. Now that one. Tell me you are at least taking advantage of having him around. I know I would."

"I'm not like that and it isn't that way between us."
*At least not yet.*

"Why not? You're single. I assume he is too, right?"

"Yes."

"Then what are you waiting on, Carly? Take action girl. Make that man yours." Margot poured the wine and handed her a glass. "If you don't someone else will."

Carly took a sip and kept quiet. She wasn't about to talk about what her relationship with Brand with Margot or any of her friends. She reached for a piece of apple and some cheese, munching on them. Margot talked about the benefits of living in the building while Carly sipped her wine.

BRAND ARRIVED at Hawkeye's district around five-thirty and went up to the conference room to get set up since that was where the driver said he should go. Hawkeye joined him a few minutes later.

"Here's a packet of the proposal and other statistics I included when I sent it for approval. I requested enough funding earmarked in next year's budget to staff at least a four-man crew for the Chicago Protection Task Force. Before the higher-ups get here I wanted to take a moment to ask if you'd consider staying in Chicago and heading this up, if it gets approved."

"Hawkeye." Brand took a breath, gripping the pages of the proposal in his hands. He loved what he was doing for Hank Patterson. He'd even grown to love living in Eagle Rock, Montana. But, having an opportunity to stay in Chicago with Carly. To run his own task force. That was something he'd not even thought about when Hawkeye started talking about forming a team to stay in the area.

"I'm honored you want me for the job."

"Why do I get the feeling there's an unsaid but coming?"

Before he could answer, four men and a woman in suits entered the room.

"We'll have to continue this later." Hawkeye left to greet the new arrivals. He shook hands with each of them before turning and motioning for Brand to join them. He did, standing at ease with his hands clasped behind his back.

"I'd like you to meet former Devgru Seal Brandon Chambers. He's part of the Brotherhood Protectors out of Eagle Rock, Montana. A four-man crew came to show how former service men and women can use their training to protect the public. Lucky for Chicago these four were here when the Pied Piper gang shooting happened. We were able to take advantage of their skills."

"From what we've seen it hasn't been successful," said the Hispanic looking man with a sharp buzz cut and graying around his temples.

Hawkeye winced and cleared his throat before he

spoke. "I admit having our witness shot at as she left Christ's Church today wasn't ideal, but we had as much security at the church as if the POTUS was visiting the area."

He pulled out a chair for the female in the group and she sat at the round table.

"And yet it failed," the man in a sharp gray suit said, taking a seat as well.

"It's unfortunate, Henry, but yes, it did. We've already taken measures to keep her safe. We reassigned her driver since his SUV also exploded today. We didn't want to take the chance that he'd been targeted and could lead the Twin Cobras to her location."

"And have you found out who got to the gang member in jail?" Brand's attention was drawn to the African American in the group.

"Surveillance footage shows that coverage lapsed for about two minutes. So no, we have no idea who got to him, but since the attack happened at the church so soon after his death we have determined that it had to be a rival gang. Why else would the Twin Cobras kill their own and still go after a witness?"

"What about the other three women that are being protected? You mentioned there were three other men here," the female said.

"What's that got to do with anything, Mona?" the African American asked.

"Everything, Terrance. We can't judge this request on one-fourth of the results. I agree with Commander

Burns what happened today is unfortunate. I don't hold him or former Devgru Seal Chambers at fault when dealing with the Twin Cobras gang. I've dealt with them in the past when I was a beat cop and then when I was a detective before I advanced into administration. They are a ruthless bunch. They are out for blood."

"I too have had dealings with this gang and what Mona says is true. Burns, I wouldn't rule out them being the ones responsible for killing their man in custody. I can see them putting a hit out on him so he wouldn't have to stand trial. I can also see them going after your witness as well."

"Thank you, Hector, for agreeing with me," Mona said. "What about you, Peter? You've stayed quiet on the matter."

"I don't see why Commander Burns believes we need to bring in military men and women to this city to do a job that our own men and women in blue could do. It appears to be a waste of budgetary money. Thus, no matter how you present it to me I am voting no."

"As counsel for the police department I have to agree."

"Henry, be reasonable," Hawkeye said. "You've heard the other members of the committee discussing it. Why won't you at least let Brand speak on the matter before you vote against the task force I'm asking to have implemented."

"Then explain why you want it from an outside source and not our own people?" Peter asked.

"Because we need our manpower on the streets doing their job, not watching over victims or witnesses. This task force can provide security details, witness protection details, you name it and they have the training to do it. It also helps many of these former service men and women use their skills in the real world when they can't find jobs otherwise."

"And what do you say former Seal Chambers?" Mona asked. "Do you believe this mission has been a waste of your time?"

"No ma'am, I don't. I've not only been keeping my witness safe from the Twin Cobras gang but also from her overprotective ex-husband who has had a P.I. tailing her. What your administrative committee doesn't know is that other than the incident at the church today, my witness has had her apartment broken into twice. Once by the P.I. to bug it for her ex-husband so he could know her every move and second by the Twin Cobras so they could trash the place and leave her a calling card of twin snakes."

Mona gasped.

"We've had to move her to a safe location not only to keep her away from the gang but from the reaches of her ex-husband. During her divorce, she couldn't get a restraining order against him due to the fact he is seen in this fine city as an aspiring attorney. His tactics are not physical but mental. But it is domestic abuse nonetheless. The judge wouldn't grant her any protection. But we will be going after it again."

"Henry, maybe you can help?" Mona asked. "It's the least we can do for our witness."

"I – I can look into it. What is the name of this witness? And the ex-husband's?"

"Carly Manning. Justin Porter."

The man stood up. "I won't sit here and listen to you spout off slanderous statements against my son-in-law. I don't care what nonsense Carly has told you."

For a split second the room was deathly quiet as everyone stared at the man and processed his outburst.

"Carly didn't have to tell me anything, sir. I saw it for myself. Ragsdale the P.I. told me what he was doing for Porter. The fact that you are more outraged over something being said about that piece of trash Porter than what has been going on with your own flesh and blood all week tells me she's far better off not having the likes of you in her life. It was hard to believe you and your wife sided with Porter over her because of the divorce, but to see it for myself..." Brand turned away from the round table where the members sat. He shook his head not believing any of this. He hoped what he said had not made the funding situation worse for Hawkeye.

"Henry, that's your daughter," Mona said. "How can you vote against this protection task force when it is providing a service to your own daughter? Not to mention side against her?"

"Mona, that's a family affair. Carly's a liar. I don't want to hear another word about it."

Brand spun around so fast he was across the room to Mr. Manning pointing his finger in his face. "No, she isn't. I've never met anyone more honest. And if you don't know that about your own daughter, then you don't deserve her in your life."

"Brand," Hawkeye was at his side, pulling him away by the arm.

Brand held up his hands and backed away. "It's okay. I'm outta here." He left the conference room and took the stairs down to the basement to the workout room. He'd learned the layout of the facility when they first arrived in Chicago.

The place was almost empty when he arrived. He taped his hands and began using the punching bag to blow off steam. Then one of the officers came in and asked if he was interested in sparring a few rounds in the ring.

He sat down on the bench and took off his shoes and socks, before joining him. They'd done this once before so he knew what he was up against. Of course, he'd not been angry that day when he'd stepped into the ring with the guy. And maybe that made the difference. He kept seeing the smarmy look on Carly's dad's face as he defended Justin Porter. That pissed Brand off even more each time as he thought about what the bastard had put Carly through. He threw a punch and the guy ducked, doing a roundabout kick that landed a blow center of his chest at his diaphragm.

He landed with a thud on his back, hitting his head on the matt. He saw flashes of Carly pass before his eyes. Images of her from the time they met up until he left her earlier that evening. And his last thought before he gasped for air with excruciating pain was there'd be no dessert tonight.

## CHAPTER 12

CARLY PACED the private surgical waiting area at Chicago Med where she and Margot waited for news on Brand. She couldn't lose him. Not now. It was too soon. They'd only found one another.

"Oh Burnsie, make her sit down. I've tried, but she refuses. All this back and forth is giving me a headache." Margot rushed to his side when he walked into the small area.

Carly looked at Margot, annoyed at her whining. "You didn't have to come when the commander called that Brand asked for me. You could have stayed at the apartment."

"What kind of a sorority sister would I have been if I let you face this alone? For all, we knew when Burnsie called is that your guy could be dying."

"There you go with 'my guy' again. He's my protector."

"Really? Just a protector wouldn't call for you to leave your secure space to come to his bedside at the hospital."

"Ladies. Please. It's been a long day. Let's all sit and wait for word on Brand. He's still being checked out in the ER."

"I'll sit, if you'll sit with me, Burnsie." Margot slipped her arm through the commanders and she looked up at him adoringly. "I've never been a fan of hospitals."

"Another reason you should have stayed at the apartment," Carly mumbled. She took a seat across from them. She'd developed a headache shortly after they arrived and the aspirin the nurse gave her hadn't taken the edge off. That was why she was finding everything Margot said or did so annoying. Not to mention her worry for Brand.

"Commander, explain to me again how this happened. I don't understand why he was kickboxing in the workout room. He left the apartment to give a demonstration with you on the task force you want to put together."

The commander went through the events leading up to Brand storming out of the meeting. She tried to ignore that Margot was hanging on the commander's arm despite the fact that he was a married man. That didn't seem to bother her friend. And bless the commander's heart. She could see it annoyed him by the glances he kept giving Margot, but her friend didn't take the hint.

"Wait. My father was there. Brand argued with my father over me?"

"Yes. The other committee members weren't happy with Henry either. When they found out he was your father and he wasn't in favor of the task force."

"And why was my father at this meeting?"

"He's been serving as counsel for the police department for the last year."

"Right." Carly nodded. "Someone in his firm has always been in charge of the police department for years. I guess it was finally his turn. So you knew my father before this?"

"Yes, but I had no idea he was your father. It never occurred to me to put attorney Henry Manning and witness Carly Manning together. Our relationship has always been professional. We've only had contact when counsel sat in on meetings. Today's meeting was the exception since it required an executive branch."

"Small world."

"Yes, it is.

The room became quiet for a few moments. Carly watched Margot tap the toe of her high heel shoe on the pale Berber carpet where she sat with the commander.

Outside in the hallway, there was a frenzy of voices that wafted through the open doorway. A red-faced nurse entered. "I'm sorry, Commander, but these people claim to know you. They refused to stay in the ER waiting area."

He stood and motioned for them to enter. "It's alright. They can join us."

Carly sucked in a breath, elated and relieved to see Jules after a week of no communication. Tears stung her eyes and she blinked them away the best she could, rushing to her friend.

Jules hugged her tight. "I've been so worried about you today ever since I saw the reports of the shooting at the church. Whatever made you go to the funeral? To risk your life like that?"

Carly pulled back and looked at Jules. "I was given the all clear to go. Besides I had to. You weren't there inside the bar when Phil was killed. Someone had to tell his wife how wonderful he was up to his last moments. If I'd been in her shoes I know I would have cherished having someone come to tell me that."

Jules hugged her again. "When we got the call tonight I knew it was about you. I never dreamed it was about Will's friend."

"I've been worried about you too. Brand hasn't had a word from Will all week. We didn't know what was going on with you."

"What? I've texted him several times, but he hasn't responded. I thought it was because all I had to report was that things were good. But you're saying he didn't get my texts?"

Carly shook her head. "He was really concerned

yesterday when we headed to my job interview."

"I wondered if you got to go. Did you get it?" Jules asked.

"No, but I was recommended to work with another designer to build up my portfolio and encouraged to apply again once I had."

"That sounds promising."

"Carly! Jules!" Simone's squeal ricocheted around the waiting area as she entered the doorway.

Carly turned in time to see her pulling Donovan behind her. She felt sorry for the guy, though he didn't look one ounce put out with Simone. In fact, he looked rather smitten.

"Oh. My. Gawd," Margot said, getting to her feet. "Simone Reid."

"Margot Wills!"

The two met in the middle of the room and did the French kiss-kiss on each cheek, and then Margot took a long look at Will and Liam up and down.

"Burnsie," Margot said, turning to the commander, pointing to the men with her index finger. "Can you get me one of these?"

"Yeah, Commander Burns, she really needs one of these," Simone chimed in, "to keep her out of trouble."

"No. And double no. I should have known the two of you knew one another. You're too much alike."

Margot and Simone giggled, hugging one another. Linking arms, the two walked over to the two-seater and sat down to talk.

Jules rolled her eyes. "How'd you run into Margot?"

Carly smiled. "It appears Commander Burns and the Senator are acquainted. I had to move out of my apartment and needed a safe place to stay so I'm temporarily in the Senator's unused place on Lakeshore."

"Fancy."

"You can say that triple times." Carly crossed her arms and hugged herself. "Was Brand able to contact Will about what happened to Colleen? Were you notified about that?"

"Yes. We did get communication. Will and Wyatt have been able to text one another and she's doing good since leaving the hospital. That is all I know and all I want to know for her safety."

"How's the budget cuts?"

"A donor stepped up at the last minute and saved us, again." Jules shook her head and sighed. "I hate these frantic periods. The kids at the youth center hate it because the staff is on edge and they can tell something is wrong. Will was a trooper. He saw me through it all. Did you know he's a fan of single-malt scotch?"

"That's great. I'm glad to hear your assigned protector has worked so well for you."

"What about Brand?" Jules asked, leaning in close. "How are things going for you? Have you gotten to use that leather teddy I gave you?"

Carly felt her face heat. "No. How could you even ask me that with him lying in the ER?"

Jules smiled and shrugged her shoulders. "Curious to know if you'd had a chance to put it to use yet."

Carly stepped away from her friend feeling self-conscious about what Jules was really trying to find out with her question about the teddy. First Margot and now Jules. It was no one else's business if Carly and Brand were in a relationship or not and right now, it was too fresh and new to discuss it with anyone.

Moving closer to the commander, she wanted to ask him another question about her father and Brand's argument, but she heard Will telling the commander about not being able to reach Brand all week.

"I haven't been able to since last Saturday either," Donovan said.

"I've had no trouble," the commander said. "Have either of you heard from Kincaid?"

They both nodded.

"I know for a fact that Brand hasn't heard from him either," Carly offered. "We discussed it on the way to my job interview. He was worried about all his men because they'd been silent."

"Carly mentioned this when Jules and I arrived so that's why I asked Donovan about it," Will said.

"Do you think someone has tampered with his phone?" Donovan asked.

The commander shook his head. "It's unlikely. He's been around very few people other than Kevin Petree and Carly all week."

"Don't forget Ragsdale," Carly said.

"But was Brand and the P.I. alone for any period of time for the man to have access to Brand's phone?"

Carly shook her head.

"What about Petree?" the commander asked. "Did you ever see Brand lay his phone down when Petree was around?"

"No, but I wasn't with them when Brand and Kevin went shopping for his suit. Kevin took him to the places he usually went and I stayed at the apartment. I can't imagine that he'd do anything to harm us. He's been so great all week."

"I'm not saying the man is guilty, I'm looking at the possibilities of who had access to Brand's phone. I'll get a tech guy down here to examine it and make sure it hasn't been tampered with so we will know for sure why the signals have been crossed."

The commander walked away and Carly felt even more unnerved by these developments, especially if it turned out that someone had tampered with Brand's phone. If the commander was right and Kevin Petree was involved in that, then she didn't want to think about what it meant about why his SUV exploded today. Had he been trying to kill her? What about the soup he'd made? She'd eaten it. Brand had too. He could have easily poisoned it if he was really out to do her harm. But why? She didn't know him from Adam. Did she?

She walked over to the cushioned seats and sat down, thinking about the possibility of having met

Kevin Petree before. He was a young detective who had come up in the ranks as a police officer. He was trusted to be a driver for the commander.

"What's wrong?" Jules asked. She sat down next to Carly and reached for her hand.

"Something the commander said about Brand's phone being tampered with that kept his team from being able to send him texts and him from sending them messages. Only three people that could have done it. Our driver, the P.I. that Justin Porter hired to watch my apartment and me."

"Justin did what?"

"It's a long story and I'll tell you about it later. But, the most likely person to have messed with Brand's phone was our driver. I was trying to recall if I had somehow met him before, but I'm coming up with nothing."

"Why would the driver want to mess with an encrypted phone?"

"How do you know the phone is encrypted?"

"Will told me because I asked."

"So whoever messed with the phone would have to have a background in computer tech, wouldn't you think?"

"Yeah or hacking skills at least."

"I think that would rule out Ragsdale. He's a former detective, but I don't think he'd have the background in that."

"Your driver was a younger guy I take it."

Carly nodded. "Around our age. Just made detective. Doing his dues driving for the commander."

Jules sighed. "Maybe he resented being giving grunt work. Instead of a real case."

"But Brand has pulled him in to help protect me. He's not been just a driver. He's actually been involved in the last two days since the Twin Cobras broke into my apartment and trashed the place. Brand and Kevin have gotten all buddy-buddy with each other and that is a big step for my guy."

"Ah ha!" Margot pointed at Carly. "So he is your guy."

"That was a figure of speech, Margot. Nothing more."

"Sure it was."

AROUND MIDNIGHT A NURSE finally came to the waiting area and took Carly down to the ER to see Brand. His eyes were closed and he was wearing an oxygen cannula at his nose when she entered the curtained off area.

"You can stay five minutes. I'll be back," the nurse said.

She reached for his hand and he slowly opened his eyes.

"Hey," he said.

"What were you trying to do?"

"Blow off some steam, but the guy I was sparring with got the better of me."

"It looks like it."

The curtain pulled back and a man stepped inside. "I'm Doctor Octavia. I've been handling Mr. Chambers' case. We've run a few tests and I can say he's very lucky. No fractured ribs after such a frontal blow to the chest. What you've experienced tonight has been agitation to the phrenic nerve due to the hit near the diaphragm. Because of your dog tags, I was able to pull your medical history and consult with your doctors at Walter Reed. I know about the shrapnel lodged near your artery. I've excellent news for you, Mr. Chambers. The shrapnel has moved. Not necessarily because of this episode, but it has moved away from the artery. We can now safely perform the surgery that caused you to be medically discharged."

"That's great. When can he have this surgery?" Carly asked.

"Wait. I think that should be up to me, don't you?" Brand said. "I'm not having any surgery until I see your mission complete."

"My mission? So, I am still just a job. Fine. Have it your way." She let go of his hand and backed away from his bedside. "If he had the surgery, how long would his recovery time be?"

"Recovery time varies from patient to patient. Six to eight weeks even for the most athletic because we do have to open up the chest."

"That's why I can't do it until after we know you are out of danger, Carly, not because you are a job. And if you can't understand that then you are being pig-headed."

"Pig-headed?"

"You heard me."

"No, we wouldn't be here tonight if you hadn't got all macho angry at my father during the meeting and had to go blow off steam in the gym."

"Did Hawkeye tell you your father was taking up for JP and downing you?"

"I figured as much."

"I wasn't going to stand by and let him do that in my presence."

Carly looked at him, lying there hooked up to the machines and the oxygen. The fact he was like this because he was protecting her honor in his own way made her forget he'd put himself in such danger. She stepped back to the bed. "I know and that's why I love you for it." She leaned down and kissed him.

"I'll let the two of you work this out. We'll be moving you to a room soon, Mr. Chambers. We're going to keep you overnight until we get your O2 stats back up."

~

BRAND WOKE the next morning expecting to find Carly sitting in the chair in the hospital room where he'd been moved, instead he found Hawkeye drinking coffee and reading a report.

"Anything interesting?"

"Very. We got the funding. We not only got the funding, but we got enough funding for six men instead of the four I requested. I've never seen that committee work so fast before, but I think after what happened yesterday seeing how Henry Manning and Peter Hastings were so dead set against it only spurred Mona Farrell, Hector Gonzalez and Terrance Blevins on, especially after they found out that Manning was opposing the Task Force even though it was helping his own daughter. That in itself may have been the deciding factor for the other three."

"We'll take the win, won't we?"

"We sure will."

"Did Carly tell you I can have surgery to get the shrapnel out now?"

"She mentioned it when I took her and Margot home. That is some news. It opens up a completely new world of opportunities for you. I was here when Dr. Octavia made his rounds this morning. I asked him the one thing that has to be going through the back of your mind. If the shrapnel is removed, does that mean you'd be cleared for active duty again."

Brand slowly raised the motorized bed so he could see Hawkeye clearer. "What did the doctor have to say about that?"

"Your doctor at Walter Reed was hopeful that with

healing and physical therapy, conditioning, and training that you'd be back up to speed and ability to pass the physical to be cleared if you so choose to return to duty. If you wanted it. Personally, I'm hoping you don't. I really want you to head up my task force and stay in Chicago. But then I'm being selfish to want you to stick around."

"No, you're not. I want to stick around too. My SEAL days are over. Getting the shrapnel out is good. I'll have the surgery as soon as we know there is no more threat to Carly's life. And to answer your question from yesterday, I'll head up your task force."

"Good. I'm glad to hear it." Hawkeye laid the report down. "There's something we need to discuss. Somehow your encrypted cellphone was hacked. That is the reason you couldn't get ahold of your team after the visit to the hospital when the girls came to see Colleen. I've confiscated it and given it to my best tech guy. He's trying to figure out what or who has touched your phone. I have my suspicions, but I need proof, solid evidence to take him down."

"I don't like the sound of this. Are you saying, Petree?"

Hawkeye nodded.

"Damn."

"Stay calm. It won't help matters for you to get upset. The doc said you need to keep your blood pressure at an even keel right now."

"Then why tell me this at all?"

"I thought you needed to know in case you go looking for your phone."

Brand shook his head. "I don't know how or when the man would have gotten access to it."

"What about when you went shopping for the suit? That is when Carly thought it might have been possible? I've had my guys looking into his background all night trying to come up with something, even the explosion on his SUV, the four tires blowing out beforehand. That seemed a little overkill to me, even for a street gang like the Twin Cobras, especially after the gunshots fired on civilians leaving Christ's church. But who knows what gangs will do when their guy in jail has just been killed."

"There is no way that a gang could retaliate that quickly for their man being taken out. I don't think the shooting or the SUV was a result of that. When have you ever known a gang to use sniper fire?"

"Never."

"And Petree told me and Carly that the guy was long gone by the time SWAT found his location. Thinking back on the chaotic scene and the timeframe it's highly unlikely that he would have been able to receive word that quickly. Yet because of the chaos, he was able to get us to go with him in his SUV since he'd been our driver."

"The factor that alludes me is the why? What would make him risk his career?"

"Or who." Brand said fiddling with the oxygen

device stuck in his nose. "Did the doc happen to say how long I had to wear this?"

"He didn't, but I wouldn't remove it since the reason he had you stay overnight was to bring up your oxygen level."

Brand sighed. "This stinks. I feel like I did when I was in Walter Reed all those weeks and I've only been here overnight."

"It can't be that bad."

"But it is. I should be at the apartment with Carly."

"Doing your job? Or spending time with your girl?"

Brand looked at him. "What do you mean?"

"You know damn well what I mean. I've never seen you lose your cool in a meeting with superiors like you did with Carly's father for taking her ex-husband's side. You've stepped over the line with this girl. You've developed feelings for her."

"So what if I have?"

"Whoa! You aren't even going to deny it. This is big. You really have feelings for her. Have the two of you gotten physical?"

"No. And if we had it wouldn't be any of your business, but we haven't. I don't want to mess things up by rushing it. She's the real deal, Hawk."

"I can see that." He nodded. "Good for you. Just be careful that you don't end up getting either one of you killed in the process. Keep your head on straight."

## CHAPTER 13

CARLY WOKE in total darkness and couldn't move her arms or legs, yet she had a sense that wherever she was at was familiar to her. The smell of the place gave her the feeling of home, but something inside didn't allow her to feel comfortable. Her hands felt numb and her wrists felt cramped. She tried flexing them, but she scraped her skin against something rough and scratchy. Swallowing, her mouth was as dry as cotton, and she began to gag because there was a rag stuffed in her mouth. Heaving for air only made matters worse and she about passed out because she couldn't get enough oxygen.

Finally, she got her breathing under control. But, she teetered to the side, falling from a sitting position to the hard floor. She hit her head on concrete. She knew without a doubt she wasn't at the senator's apartment nor was she at her small apartment across town.

The familiar smell of home made her think of the basement at her parents' house. Another whiff reminded her of the unfinished storage space off from the garage at the house she'd shared with Justin Porter. That made her sick to her stomach.

It was impossible for her to be at either house, wasn't it? She'd left the hospital with Margot and Commander Burns in the early morning hours after Brand had been moved into a room. The commander had driven them to the Lakeshore apartment building and seen them to their respective floors before leaving. At least Carly assumed Margot had allowed the man to leave. She had been so clingy last night. Surely, Margot didn't act like that when her father was around.

The commander had handed Carly the keys to the apartment and she'd sent the elevator back down to Margot's floor before she went into the apartment, locking the door. She took a quick shower, put on her pajamas and crawled into bed where she fell asleep. She remembered all that clearly.

What she didn't remember is how she ended up here.

The sound of heavy footsteps drew her attention away from her thoughts. She listened intently wondering if the person was coming toward her. The ringing of a phone sent the footsteps in the opposite direction.

The whoosh of water flowing through pipes was the next sound she heard and then a squeak and scurry of little feet along the cement floor. Carly's mind began to race with vivid images of tiny creatures eating away at her flesh and she cringed, trying to push those thoughts away as fast as they came to her. She had almost succeeded when she thought she heard the sound of hissing and she lost it and screamed the best she could against the gag in her mouth. However, only muffled sounds came out and she soon was out of breath and heaving for air before she lost consciousness.

It was around noon when Dr. Octavia sent around orders that Brand could go home once his O2 stats reached above normal status. The head nurse on his floor brought him the news herself.

"Will you have someone to pick you up?" she asked.

"I'll get someone here. Don't worry."

"Your t-shirt was destroyed last night in the ER. I've brought you a Chicago Med shirt to replace it. I hope an XL will do?"

"Thanks."

"Buzz if you need anything."

Once she left, Brand didn't waste time changing out of the hospital gown back into his street clothes. He put the oxygen back on and sat on the bed while he dialed Hawkeye's number.

"Burns."

"Brand. I'm being released. I'll need a ride to the Lakeshore apartment if you can swing it."

"Great, but how about you come by the department and let's go over some task force stats first? Since you aren't that far away. I'll give Margot a call and have her drop in on Carly if she hasn't already today."

"Okay. Sure. Work does come first."

"I won't keep you long. An hour at most."

"What about the situation we were talking about earlier? Any news on that?"

"Negative, but I will make a few follow up calls. I've been snowed under since I got in this morning. I'll see you soon."

Brand hung up the phone and leaned back in bed waiting for the nurse to return and check his O2 stats again and tell him he could leave. He counted the ceiling tiles twice and then reached for the phone trying to recall Carly's cell phone number. He'd called her on it once and he was pretty sure he remembered the number. He took a stab at it and listened as the call went through ringing three then four times before getting her voice mail.

"Hey Carly, it's Brand. Just wanted to let you know I'm coming home. I mean…getting out of the hospital. I'll be back this afternoon after stopping by Chicago PD for a briefing on the new task force. We got the funding and Hawkeye has asked me to head up the team. Isn't that great? We can talk more about what this means when I see you. I don't have my cell right now, but you can call the hospital and see if I'm still here if you want. You know the room number."

He hung up, then placed the phone back on the stand beside the bed. He took the oxygen out of his nose and walked over to the window, staring out into the city.

"Mr. Chambers, did I tell you that you could get out of bed?" the head nurse asked coming into the room.

"No, but I was bored lying there."

"Come here and let me check your stats if you want to get out of here." The woman peered at him over the edge of her bifocals. She placed the Pulse Oximeter on the end of his finger and waited for it to beep with a reading. "Very good. Looks like I can let you sign these discharge papers after all."

He took the clipboard and pen, scratching his name across the signature line with the fine point tip. "I can't say this hasn't come a moment too soon. I was contemplating making a break for it."

The woman grinned. "Then you won't like the wheelchair that has been ordered to take you downstairs."

"I can walk."

"That's what they all say, but regulations call that patients be wheeled out of the hospital."

He crossed his arms and looked her in the eye. "How 'bout we say you did and I don't tell."

She grunted and shook her head. "Cheeky devil. Get out of here."

"Thank you, ma'am."

He was half-way to the door when the phone rang. He stopped, pivoted to get it thinking it was Carly calling him back. "Hello."

"Brand, my cars downstairs."

"I was on my way down, Hawkeye."

"Good. We have a situation."

## CHAPTER 14

Brand rode to the Lakeshore apartments in silence. He replayed what Hawkeye told him about how Carly had vanished without a trace during the night. How Carly didn't answer her phone and she wasn't there when Margot went to check on her. So the woman let herself into the apartment with the second set of keys to the apartment she possessed. That she hadn't told him she had.

"How did this happen if you still had plainclothes detectives stationed downstairs?" he asked.

"The night security guard got suspicious of them hanging around in the lobby. They moved to their vehicle, but they were still on the case."

"So anyone could have entered and left the building without them being the wiser. Do you know how many entrances there are to that building? Petree and I scouted that place out the day we moved in. It is not a secure place; no wonder the senator had the 20th-floor key protected."

"You and Petree?"

Brand nodded. "Damn. You don't think he's behind this, do you? What did you find out about his background? My phone?"

"We're keeping your phone as evidence." Hawkeye reached into his suit pocket and pulled out a phone. "Here's one like it. My tech guy programmed in essential numbers like McLeod, Donovan and Kincaid's as well as mine."

"Hanks?"

Hawkeye nodded. "A CSI team is at the apartment going over it with a fine brush to see if they can lift any prints. If Carly left against her will we will find her."

"You know she did. She wouldn't leave the safety of the apartment for any other reason. Where would she go? She has no one other than Jules, Simone, and Colleen, that she can trust. Her parents turned their backs on her when she decided to divorce Justin Porter."

"I know you think you have gotten to know Carly very well, but what if there are things about her that you don't know?"

Brand shook his head. "No. Don't try to play that card. You never did answer my question about Petree. What did you find out about his background?"

"There's a tie between him and Justin Porter. They belonged to the same fraternity at the same time. Carly didn't recognize him. So it doesn't mean that the two men knew one another."

"Not necessarily. Carly may not have known him, but that doesn't mean that Porter and Petree weren't acquainted. From what I gather, fraternities are breeding grounds for brotherhoods much like the military. The two wouldn't have to be besties to be tight."

"So you think there could still be a connection."

"Hell yeah."

CARLY WOKE to the smell of something frying with garlic and tomato, a little basil and oregano thrown in the mix. It made her stomach rumble. She tried to ignore the savory scent because she knew she wasn't going to be getting any of it. She didn't even know if the fragrance was coming from where she'd heard the footsteps before or from somewhere nearby.

Still lying on the cold concrete, her cheek felt numb now as did her arm, wrist, and leg on her right side. She tried to roll to her stomach and then to her other side and her back. She was in a large enough space that she was able to move freely. Now if she could only manage to get to the wall she might be able to push against it and get to a sitting position again.

A loud hissing sound and something springing against a cage stopped her from moving. She'd forgotten about the strange sounds she'd heard earlier before she'd passed out. This time the hissing sounding more like that of a mad cat in a cage than twin cobra snakes. Who knew what she was hearing or if she was right about the space where she was rolling around. She rolled back to her stomach and decided to try to inch herself up from there like an inchworm and see if she could get to her knees and maybe her feet.

She'd succeeded in getting herself scrunched enough to push her butt up in the air when the door to the room opened. Through the blindfold, she sensed the change in lighting. She froze unsure if she was being seen or not.

"Here kitty, kitty," a woman called, shuffling into the room. "Nice kitty."

The cage rattled as Carly imagined the woman opened it up to put the food inside. The cat hissed and lunged against the side because of the racket the cage made. The woman stumbled backward, bumping into shelving, letting out a shriek.

"Damn cat. I don't get paid enough to deal with you."

The door slammed closed and the light disappeared. Carly relaxed and slumped against the floor, prostrate again. The woman hadn't seen her at all yet she could sense the light filter into the room? How could that have been? Where was she with a cat that smelled familiar? Justin Porter never had a cat. He hated them as far as she knew.

MARGOT GREETED Brand and Hawkeye when they arrived at the apartment. The CSI unit was packing up. Hawkeye spoke with the one in charge about what their findings looked like before he walked them to the elevator.

"What do you make of this?" Brand asked Margot. "Has anyone ever broken in here before while your father has lived here?"

The woman shook her head, sipping on a glass of red wine even though it was early afternoon. "Strangest thing I've seen. The only way to get up that elevator is with a key to this floor and unless you have that passkey, you aren't getting up here. Either that or landing on the roof. Helicopters aren't cheap. Do you think her abductor has money?"

"Justin Porter does."

"Brand, you can't go jumping to conclusions or making accusations without evidence," Hawkeye said, returning to the apartment.

"He wouldn't do it himself. He'd hire someone to do it for him. He wouldn't get his hands dirty. Just like he's had a P.I. watching her apartment probably ever since she moved in. And until I came on the scene she didn't have a clue the P.I. was out there."

"Shit," Margot said, sitting down her glass of wine. "I knew Justin Porter was a douche bag in college, but I had no idea he'd fallen that low."

"You knew him?" Hawkeye asked.

"Sure I did. Our sorority and his fraternity did events together. That's how he caught Carly's eye. And he's the reason Carly and I lost touch. Once she started dating him he made certain she didn't have contact with many of her friends. But I guess he couldn't break the tie between Carly, Jules, Simone, and Colleen."

Brand looked at Hawkeye and raised his brows.

"Would you happen to know if Justin and this man were friends?" Hawkeye asked showing Margot a picture of Kevin Petree.

She grinned big. "Oh, you mean Petree Metree. Sure. They were thick as thieves, though Petree looks very different now than he did back then. He wore wire-rimmed glasses, had a bad case of acne that still hadn't gone away, but it didn't matter. His family was loaded and he was a legacy to his frat house so he was a yes pledge from the get-go. He was quite nerdy looking in those days too. What's he do now?"

"He's a detective."

"Really?" Margot sounded interested. "He's really done well for himself, better than I ever expected."

"You didn't see him around last night did you?" Brand asked.

"No."

"Anything else you can think of to tell us about him?" Hawkeye said.

Margot thought for a moment then shook her head.

"Thanks for your help."

"Wait, one more question," Brand said. "If you knew him right away when you saw his photo, then why do you suppose Carly didn't recognize him?"

Margot winked at them. "Because Simone and I got around more than sweet Carly and Colleen ever did, that's why. We partied with the frat boys."

Brand nodded. "So what you're really saying is that Porter and Petree were friends, but they were more in the frat house buddy buddies than they were outside the frat house friends?"

"Exactly. You've heard the phrase what happens in Vegas stays in Vegas. Well, it probably originated in a frat house. What happens in a frat house stays in a frat house." Margot took another sip of her wine, draining the glass. "I'm not saying that Porter was cruel or acted like he didn't know Petree in public, but he didn't act like they were as close. Petree was cool. He knew his place and went with it as if he preferred staying in the background. I always thought that a little odd, but who was I to question it always having to be in the spotlight being a politician's daughter growing up."

"You have given us excellent information, Margot," Hawkeye said.

"For you, Burnsie, I will do anything. You know that. In return, just find Carly. That poor girl just wants a normal life again. She has an appointment this afternoon to look at the apartment on the eighth floor that will be vacant soon. It'll be nice to have her living so close to me."

"When did she decide this?" Brand asked.

"Last night while you were off doing your presentation. We were having cheese and wine and she mentioned loving it here and I told her about the soon to be vacancy. I made a phone call this morning before I knew she was missing and arranged for her to see the apartment."

"But she has a place."

Margot shook her head. "She said she can't go back there after what happened. She needed to start fresh and she liked it here."

Brand crossed his arms over his chest. He couldn't complain that it was a far better neighborhood than her previous address, but how was she going to afford the rent. Had she gotten the job with Brittany Daniels and not mentioned it to him?

"Good. I'm glad she's thinking of her future once this is over," he said.

"It's a two bedroom, much like this one, if you are interested in knowing," Margot added.

He nodded.

"Plenty of room for two."

Brand didn't acknowledge that last part and he could tell that it irritated the woman, she tapped her painted nail on the kitchen counter in a rhythmic beat.

"I think he gets your meaning, Margot."

"Good, because he's unreadable."

Brand smirked and crossed his arms over his chest. "It doesn't take much to ruffle your feathers."

Hawkeye's phone buzzed and he took the call, walking away from them to the wall to ceiling glass windows. When he turned around he announced, "We have a fingerprint match from the bedroom. I take it that Petree was never in the bedroom when you were moving in?"

"Never. I carried Carly's things in there. He only handled the kitchen items."

"Then we got him. CSI lifted a full print off the night table. They also found a bottle of chloroform in the dumpster out back with his fingerprints on it as well. Now to figure out where he took Carly."

"You better reschedule the appointment to see the apartment to another day," Brand said. "Just to be on the safe side."

Margot nodded.

"Is he at work today?"

Hawkeye nodded. "He's been assigned to desk duty for a while because of the SUV explosion. I'm calling his supervisor now to detain him until we get there."

"My tactical bag? Is it still in the conference room?"

"Yes."

"I need to retrieve it when we get to the station."

"You do that." Hawkeye held up a finger, turned slightly away and spoke into his phone. "What do you mean he went to lunch and never returned? I need you to put out an APB on him now. Just do it. He's a man of interest in a case and we need to find him ASAP. It's a matter of life and death. Do I make myself clear? I'll be

at the station in ten minutes. I want an update immediately."

BRAND RETRIEVED his tactical bag and met up with
Hawkeye in his office back at the police station. Detectives and police sergeants were coming and going as
plans were being put into place. All known address for
Kevin Petree and his parents were pulled and cruisers
were being sent to those locations as were the home of
Justin Porter to be on the safe side.

When Brand walked into the office, Hawkeye was
on the phone with Henry Manning. He explained that
someone abducted Carly in the middle of the night
from the safe house and he was doing everything
within his power to find her. "The good news is we
believe we know who has her so it is just a matter of
time until we get her back."

"No. I am not accusing her ex-husband. I did not
say anything about him being involved. It's someone
else in fact. We have a fingerprint that puts the suspect
at the scene so we know for a fact it isn't her ex-
husband."

There was a pause before Hawkeye spoke again. "I
thought you needed to know what was going on with
your daughter, Henry. The Chicago PD is doing everything we can do to get her back to you safe and sound."

"No. He was in the hospital all night. Remember, he

was injured in a sparring match in the gym when we went downstairs after the meeting. The EMTs were loading him into the ambulance. So, he couldn't protect her. In fact, now that you mention it that seems like the perfect excuse for Carly to have not been protected. What if that wasn't an accidental injury at all? Thanks, Henry, you may have opened up another line of investigation without knowing it."

Hawkeye ended one call and he immediately placed another. He motioned for Brand to sit down while the phone rang. He spoke to the trainer on duty in the gym about the log sign in. It didn't take him long to find out the officer's name, Spencer Kirkland, who sparred with Brand in the ring. Then he called Kirkland's unit supervisor. Several phone calls later, Burns had talked to fellow officers that the man worked. He was able to make a connection between Kirkland and Petree.

"It's a thin line, but enough of one that if we work it right, we could get the two to turn on each other. All we need to do is make one believe the other is getting immunity first."

"Now what? I can't sit here waiting for the word to come in that your people have something. I need to be out there searching for Carly."

"And we will, but we need to make sure all bases have been covered first. We don't need to waste our time running around town when we can pinpoint the likely spot she is at from here."

"But what if she is being held where she has only so much air and time is running out?"

"There would have been a ransom if that was the case. Besides, this is Porter using Petree to do his dirty work just like you said. He doesn't want to hurt Carly. He wants to control her. She got away from him when she moved away from her apartment and he couldn't have his P.I. watching her. So he had to swoop in and snatch her away from the Lakeshore apartment."

"I thought you said I couldn't go making accusations without evidence?"

"I did, but the way Henry immediately went to Porter's defense when I called him. He wasn't concerned about his daughter. He was more concerned for Porter being falsely accused of her abduction. That just burns my biscuits."

## CHAPTER 15

CARLY LISTENED to the cat finish the food and then purr appreciatively. When the sound became muffled, she assumed it was because the cat was bathing its paws. She rolled to her side and her back again until she came to a wall and tried to wiggle herself to a sitting position, not allowing her mind to play tricks on her this time. She assured herself that the hissing sound she'd heard earlier had been the cat, not a cobra snake. The scurry of little feet may have been a mouse, but she was certain the cat had taken care of it straight away if it got near its cage. Maybe that was why there had been the hissing in the first place.

Rocking herself, she used her hips and legs to manage to get to a sitting position finally. In her efforts, she also dislodged the blindfold covering her eyes, so it was askew and she could see a little light now. Using her legs and her bottom, she scooted the best she could until she came to what felt like a structure at her side, but it wasn't sturdy. It gave way with her and the cat began screeching and hissing, making an awful noise that hurt her ears.

It didn't take long for the door to be flung open and a flood of light to return to the room.

"Mon Dieu!" the woman who'd fed the cat said.

For some reason Carly imagined the woman crossing herself, but she pushed those thoughts out of her mind. She had to get her to help her. If only she could spit the wad of fabric out of her mouth, but it too was tied around her face so it wouldn't come out.

She tried making groaning sounds to draw the woman's attention to her mouth and she rocked back and forth, trying to entreat her to come forward. Instead, the woman slammed the door and Carly heard her footsteps retreating quickly from the room.

Why? Why wouldn't the woman try to help her?

Anger rose up in her chest and that made Carly determined to get free on her own. The woman had opened the door twice without unlocking it. She'd come in freely. That meant the only way Carly was being held was by her bindings. If she could get her hands free, then she could get her ankles free and escape on her own.

*If the woman hasn't reported to finding Carly being awake to someone.*

That was a chance she'd have to take if she wanted to get out of here.

She had to get out of here. She had to get to Brand. He was hurt and in the hospital. He didn't even know she was missing. No one knew she was missing.

That thought spurred her on. She was more determined to get out of there than she had been before to get back to Brand.

THE OFFICER that Brand had sparred with the night before was detained from leaving the building after his shift ended. A detective questioned him about a routine traffic stop he'd made earlier that day. They were in open view as Kevin Petree was walked through the station into an interrogation room. From Brand's viewpoint, it was clear that Petree saw the detective questioning Kirkland. The murderous look that crossed his face proved that Hawkeye's point was made. Petree assumed that the officer was spilling what he knew on him.

Both Brand and Hawkeye watched and listened at the window as detectives questioned Petree about Carly Manning. He didn't budge at first. He played it cool, pretending he knew nothing about her once he was reassigned. He didn't even flinch when the detective revealed the fingerprint matches in the bedroom and on the chloroform bottle.

Brand walked away half an hour into the interrogation. He knew it could go on for hours before the perp would crack. There had to be a way to speed things up. He walked across the room to where the detective was still chatting about the routine stop.

*Boy, that detective must be good if he can keep this one on the hook with that bull this long.*

"Sorry to interrupt," he said.

"Not a problem. We were finished," the detective said. He stood and left his desk.

"Good to see you up and about. Sorry about last night. I didn't mean to take you out and send you to hospital."

"It's all good. It was an accident, right? It wasn't like you did it on purpose?"

"Right."

"Unfortunately, your buddy in there is throwing you under the bus."

"My buddy?"

"Petree."

"Who do you mean?"

"Kevin Petree. Come on. Don't play dumb with me. I know you know him. He told me all about how you two were friends when he was driving me around. You must have really done something to piss him off for him to turn on you like this."

"What's he saying?"

"You know. How you're the one that broke in and kidnapped Carly Manning for Justin Porter last night."

"He what?" Kirkland said loudly drawing the attention of others around them. "I had nothing to do with that. No way, man. He ain't pinning that shit on me. I helped him take you out, but that is it. Nothing else. He wanted me to help him do the job last night, but I told him you were a one-time deal."

"Is that so?" Hawkeye asked arriving in time to hear it all. "And just how did he persuade you to injure Brand for him? Was there money involved, Officer Kirkland?"

Kirkland got to his feet. "No, Commander. There wasn't money involved. I owed him a favor and this was to clean the slate."

"Did he tell you where he was taking her?" Brand asked.

"No. Once I refused to take part that was the end of the discussion."

Hawkeye nodded. He picked up a clipboard off of the detective's desk with a sheet of paper that looked to contain a good paragraph of typed text with a line underneath for a signature. "Here, sign this."

"Why?"

"Just do it if you don't want to lose your job." Hawkeye held the clipboard for the man to sign. "Okay, Kirkland. You hang on here. Brand, come with me."

Hawkeye went to the closed interrogation door and knocked. The door opened and he went in, holding up the clipboard.

"I have a signed statement here from Kirkland. He's confessed to his involvement. So we know you took her. Where is she, Petree?"

"We know you took her, Petree Metree. So you might as well tell us or do I need to persuade you?" Brand said, stepping around Hawkeye to look the man in the eye. "Not one hair on her head had better be harmed. Do you hear me?"

CARLY SLUMPED against the wall and felt like crying in frustration. In all her efforts, she'd gotten the blindfold all the way off, but that was all. Now she was exhausted. Her tailbone hurt from sitting on the hard concrete floor for so long and she was getting a chill. Not to mention she was hungry and she really needed to go to the bathroom.

In the distance, she thought she heard the faint sound of a siren, but she didn't pay attention to it. She'd given up hope of hearing the sound of someone coming for her all day. She closed her eyes and imagined Brand holding and kissing her the way he had after they moved into the apartment and again after the funeral service. She could almost feel him close as she thought about him and then she recalled how he'd been when they first met. He'd been so gruff and hard around the edges, but he'd soon softened. Had she done that to him?

The sirens were closer and grew louder and louder. The cat hissed, jumped on the side of the cage, and then let out a hair-raising yawl. Why would anyone keep a creature in a cage like that; in a room like this? No wonder the cat was acting feral.

Those thoughts hadn't run through her head until she heard running of feet pounding on the pavement close by. Then someone ordered, "Go. Go. Go."

The door to the room flew open, flooding the space with light. The cat meowed at an octave so sharp it pierced Carly's ears. Then the light vanished as the frame of Brand filled the doorway.

"Carly!" He called as soon as he spotted her, crossing the distance to her.

She attempted to scoot toward him, but he reached her before she made any progress. He had the gag untied and out of her mouth immediately and she gasped for air, sweet, unencumbered air.

"Thank heavens. There is a deranged cat in a cage over there. Someone needs to save it."

"Don't worry about the cat. Let's get you out of here," Brand said. He made quick work of unfettering her wrists and then her ankles. Rubbing her wrists vigorously he brought circulation back before he scooped her up and carried her outside her dungeon.

"Where am I anyway?" she asked. "I had a sense of familiarity for some reason, but I don't recognize this place at all."

"Are you sure?" Brand asked. He stood for a moment and let her take a good long look around until he heard her gasp.

"The country club."

"You said it. You spent how many days here when you were married?"

"More than I could count, but I was never down here. Near the kitchen area. I was always up at the dining area."

An ambulance pulled up and the EMTs came running over with a gurney. Brand put her on it.

"I don't need to go to the hospital."

"You need to be checked out. We know when you were abducted chloroform was used. We need to know if any other substance was used."

A black SUV pulled up and Hawkeye got out on one side followed by Henry Manning on the other.

"What's he doing here?" Carly said as one of the paramedics cuffed her to take her blood pressure.

"I'll find out," Brand said. He stepped away to inquire why Manning was there. He started to ask when Hawkeye shook his head, so he remained silent.

"So this is where Petree brought her?" Henry Manning said. "Peculiar place to hide her."

"Very, especially since this is the one place that Justin Porter insisted that Carly represents him as his dutiful wife. This is where she had to be her best for him. Why do you suppose anyone would bring her here unless there was a connection to Porter? Or they were trying to get Porter's attention." Hawkeye shook his head. "I can't make heads nor tails of it. What do you make of it, Henry?"

"I find it a set up. Petree was Carly's driver. She

could have told him she belonged to this country club and how Justin's family were founding members tying him to the place."

"But she didn't," Brand said. "This is the first I'm hearing about Porter's family being founding members. I've been with Carly every minute that she was with Petree since he was our driver. They didn't really converse with one another."

"Actually, that's false, Mr. Chambers. You haven't been with my daughter every minute she was with Petree in the vehicle. Remember, you got out at the corner before her job interview at Stella Stone Interior Designs building."

"Now how did you know that, Henry?" Hawkeye asked.

"I – I."

"Don't say any more. It'll be less incriminating. You may want to contact an attorney, you'll need one," Hawkeye said, reaching under his suit jacket and producing a pair of handcuffs. He slipped them on Manning's wrists. "One more thing, Porter, he was behind this, right?"

Manning nodded.

"That's all I needed to know," Hawkeye said, leading him passed Carly on the gurney as the paramedics worked with her.

"Daddy?" Carly said. "Brand, what's going on?"

"He apparently knew about what was going on,

whether he was involved or not, he could be charged with collusion."

"Oh, Daddy."

"We're going to load her into the bus now," one of the paramedics said.

Brand stepped away and let them do their job. "I'll see you at the hospital in a few when this is over."

"Okay."

He waited until the bus pulled away before he went to the SUV and got in with Hawkeye before they headed across town to pay a visit to Porter's law firm. He didn't know what he expected would happen when he finally came face to face with Porter. The man was everything he imagined he'd be and more. Charm and arrogance. Brand decided to stand clear while the officers with them did their job. The last thing Carly needed right now was for him to lose his head and be thrown into jail for assault against her ex-husband.

When Porter walked by him in handcuffs he halted and sneered at him. "She's used goods you know. I had her first."

"Her name is Carly and she's a human being, not a possession. No one owns her."

"Get him out of here," Hawkeye ordered. He slapped Brand on the back. "Good restraint, buddy."

The two took a different elevator down as the officers and Porter before they headed to the hospital to check up on Carly. She was sitting in the waiting room with a blanket wrapped around her and a pair of scruffy socks on her feet. She slowly stood when she saw Brand and a smile spread across her face.

She ran to him, dropping the blanket along the way and he caught her in his arms. "Is it over? Did you get him this time?"

"Porter has been arrested. Hawkeye slapped the handcuffs on him. He should be at the station getting booked."

"Finally. But what if a judge throws it out as no evidence like my other claims of domestic violence."

"That won't happen, Carly. You were kidnapped. We have Petree. We have your father on collusion. And, we have Porter. Hell, if I wanted to get technical, I could even arrest Ragsdale for doing his job as a PI for Porter, but I'll use him as a witness instead. We'll make this case stick."

"And the Twin Cobras?" she asked.

"There shouldn't be a threat from them anymore since their man in custody was killed, but you've got Brand by your side. And we'll continue to keep a watch out on our end."

"Good. Because I'm tired of all this looking over my shoulder every time I go out. I want to be able to relax. Just go back to the apartment and take a good long shower and eat a steak."

"Oh, you do?" Brand said.

She nodded. "You up to grilling?"

"I think that can be arranged. I got a good deal on some last week."

## CHAPTER 16

CARLY STOOD under the showerhead letting the hot water run over her. There was bruising starting to show around her wrists and ankles from the bindings. She yawned, closing her eyes, and leaned her forehead against the tile. Letting her body relax with the flow of the water, she almost missed the sound of the door opening and that she was no longer alone.

"Do you always walk in on a girl's privacy like this?" she asked.

"No, but I thought in your case I'd make an exception since you're taking so long."

She giggled and reached her hand behind her for him to take. He did and she brought him closer. "My neck is sore. My tailbone is sore from scooting around on that floor all day, trying to get my wrists untied."

"That's terrible." He stood behind her and began kissing her shoulders, up her neck, and then he began to massage her neck with his fingers, kneading gently. He trailed his fingers down her spine, kneading and prodding and went back to kissing her neck. When he hit the middle of her back, one spot sent a thousand sensations rippling down to her toes and she groaned. He continued his administrations there for the longest.

"How's that feel?" he asked, huskily.

"Amazing." All thoughts of her sore tailbone were gone.

"Now turn around."

She did, slowly wiping the water from her face and eyes as she stepped from under the showerhead. As soon as she did, he captured her mouth with his and claimed her. She wrapped her arms around his neck as he lifted her up, pressing her against the cool, wet tile of the shower. She wrapped her legs around his waist, as she slid into perfect position against him.

She broke away from their kissing and looked at him, breathless. "I know I'm alive, Brand. I'm not trying to prove anything, except how much I want to be with you. Not just for this moment, but for as long as you want to be with me."

"I know that, Carly. I want that too."

She leaned in to kiss him again and he carried her out of the shower into the bedroom, where she noticed the room glowed in candlelight. He'd already turned down the bedsheets so there was no awkwardness when he laid her down. She understood why he said she was taking too long in the shower now. Without her knowing, he'd been waiting out here for her to join him and that made her smile as she accommodated his weight. He reached for something on the bedside table and laid it beside them.

"You want the handcuffs and whip too?" he asked, arching his brows.

"What?" she turned her head slightly and saw the condom wrapper. How had he found her stash from the Pied Piper? Had he been searching her closet for them? "No, those aren't necessary."

"Good, because I want you touching me." He dipped his head and captured her mouth for another soul searing kiss that left her breathless. She tried to catch her breath as he moved down to her breasts, nipping and suckling one and then the other until she was wet with desire for him. His hand stroked and caressed as it moved down her stomach to her hip to her mound before he slipped his finger inside her wet haven.

Even though she had anticipated his touch, it had sent shock waves through her when he entered the juncture, jolting her. She grabbed for the condom and tore the packet open with her teeth. He looked up and grinned.

"That anxious?"

Carly nodded, unable to form words at the magic his hands had performed on her body. She watched as he sat back, putting on the condom before he covered her body with his own and they finally made love for the first time. It was hard, it was intense, but it was also cleansing. With her climax came the peace she had been searching for and she wept. Brand held her afterward, kissing her gently, and whispering sweet words that everything was going to okay. For the first time in a long time, she truly felt loved.

Committing herself to another man may not come easy after what she'd been through with Justin Porter. But, Carly knew that Brand wanted to be with her and she wanted to be with him. For now, that was enough. It was a stepping stone they could build upon.

WAKING FIRST THE NEXT MORNING, Carly showered and dressed, before she went into the kitchen. She finally made the overdue phone call to Brittany Daniels, praying with each ring that the position was still open.

"Brittany Daniels Designs."

"May I speak to Ms. Daniels? My name is Carly Manning. She is expecting a call from me."

"You are and I have. Thank you for finally calling. Stella Stone said you'd be calling. When you didn't phone immediately, I thought you had thought better of it. But then Stella said she'd heard you were in that incident at Christ's Church the other day."

"I was. I do apologize for the delay in calling. I have been literally tied up since then. I'd like to meet you and show you my design portfolio and see if you are interested in working with me. That is if the job is still open. I totally understand if you have already filled the position because of my tardiness in calling."

"The job is open and the job is yours. I trust Stella explicitly. If she says you're my designer then I take her word for it. When can you start?"

Carly blinked. This was way too easy and she didn't know if she liked it. She'd rather know she got the job because Brittany looked at her designs and liked what she saw than taking Stella's word for it. "Are you sure you don't want to meet first, maybe for coffee and make sure our personalities mesh? What if you hate me?"

"I couldn't hate you, Ms. Manning. Anyone who would worry about our personalities clashing is the very person I want to work with, but if you insist on a meeting, let us do coffee this afternoon say two at Jaboo's. Are you familiar with it?"

"Yes."

"Excellent. Bring your portfolio along and I'll take a look at it. And we can talk particulars."

"Perfect. Thank you, Ms. Daniels."

"Call me, Brittany."

"See you at two, Brittany."

Carly hung up and went back into the bedroom to wake Brand, but the bed was empty. She heard the water running, so she made the bed and straightened up the room from the night before while she waited on him to tell him her good news. Things were looking up. Now if she only had a place to call home again.

She went back to the living room and called Margot to find out when she'd scheduled a tour of the apartment on the eighth floor.

"Carly Manning, thank God you are alive. Do you know I was worried sick? You could have called me last night to tell me you were home safe. Instead, I had to hear it from Burnsie."

"Sorry. I had other things on my mind last night."

"I'm sure you did. All six foot of Brand."

"Listen, about the apartment on the eighth floor. Is it still an option to see it sometime today? I have a two o'clock appointment, but I'm free the rest of the day."

"I had you scheduled yesterday, but I had to cancel because you were abducted. I can't just snap my fingers and make it happen again that easy. But I will call and see if it is possible for later today or tomorrow. In the meantime, I'll pick up an application from the rental office downstairs for you to fill out. Get your name in for consideration before there is a list for a vacancy."

"Okay. Thanks. And sorry to be such a pain. I didn't set out to get abducted. You know that."

"I know. We should all live such exciting lives."

Carly snorted at her snark. "I'll try to tone it down."

"You should. Humdrum has been more of your style."

"Gee thanks."

"So how was Brand?"

"None of your business."

"That good, huh?"

"Good-bye, Margot."

"Ta-ta."

~

"WHO WAS THAT?" Brand came into the room wearing a towel wrapped around his waist as he headed toward the back bedroom.

"Margot. I was checking on an apartment on the eighth floor that is coming open. I want to see it. I was thinking about relocating to a better neighborhood with my new job prospect."

"That's an excellent idea. It's also close to the district for me."

She got up and followed him down the hallway. "Do you know yet if the funding has been approved?"

"Yes. Sorry. I forgot to tell you last night. Hawkeye's proposal was approved with more funding for two extra men than the four he wanted. So I will have a team of five under me."

"Great. Do you know where the unit will be located? Will you be at a specific police district?"

"Hawkeye didn't say, but with it being his baby I'd assume it would be located in his district."

"You shouldn't assume. Find out for sure where and then decide the best location for your apartment."

"Even if that isn't here?"

She nodded. "We can always look elsewhere if needed. I haven't a clue yet what the rent will be and I have to find out what my salary will be from Brittany Daniels when I meet with her this afternoon at two. I might not be able to afford the rent here."

"You mean we might not be able to afford it."

"I didn't want to just assume we'd live together, even if I do want to be with you."

"Then move in with me, Carly, let's be together for real. I've never been with anyone like this before and think it's because I was waiting for the right person to come into my life. You are the right one, Carly. I knew it when I walked into that bar and saw you wearing the cute little leather short shorts and those silver studded boots."

She smiled, running her hand up his bare chest to rest at his heart. "You don't think we're moving too fast? My divorce was just finalized even though I'd been legally separated for two years. I really do feel like I'm ready to move on."

"Who cares about the timing? Your marriage was way over before you ever separated. Who among your friends will question your actions? Your parents won't care."

Carly thought about that for a moment. All her friends wanted was for her to be happy and Brand made her happy. As for her parents …well they lost their say when they sided with Justin Porter.

"It's a two bedroom. We'll take it slow, giving each other space. We'll play it by ear if that makes you feel better."

She nodded. "Yes, living together sounds perfect."

Brand tilted her chin up and kissed her. She rose up on her tiptoes and kissed him back; opening her mouth, her heart and her soul to him and the future, they would build together.

ORIGINAL BROTHERHOOD PROTECTORS
SERIES

BY ELLE JAMES

## ABOUT ELLE JAMES

ELLE JAMES also writing as MYLA JACKSON is a *New York Times* and *USA Today* Bestselling author of books including cowboys, intrigues and paranormal adventures that keep her readers on the edges of their seats. With over eighty works in a variety of sub-genres and lengths she has published with Harlequin, Samhain, Ellora's Cave, Kensington, Cleis Press, and Avon. When she's not at her computer, she's traveling, snow skiing, boating, or riding her ATV, dreaming up new stories. Learn more about Elle James at www.elle-james.com

Website | Facebook | Twitter | GoodReads | Newsletter | BookBub | Amazon

*Follow Elle!*
www.ellejames.com
ellejames@ellejames.com

facebook.com/ellejamesauthor
twitter.com/ElleJamesAuthor

Made in the USA
Coppell, TX
18 April 2023

15779735R00125